FURTHER TALES FROM SPACESHIP EARTH

FURTHER TALES FROM SPACESHIP EARTH

Blue Marble Space Institute of Science
Short Story Collection
Volume 2

Edited by H. James Cleaves and Palmer Fliss

Habitable Press

Blue Marble Space Institute of Science
http://www.bmsis.org

Cover design by Michigan-based artist Lis Borris.
http://lizzie-bean.com

Printed in the United States of America
First Printing: August 2017

Published by Habitable Press
1001 4th Ave, Suite 3201, Seattle WA 98154, USA
http://habitablepress.org

ISBN-10: 0692855262
ISBN-13: 978-0692855263
LCCN: 2017935689

"We are called to be architects of the future,
not its victims."

Buckminster Fuller

CONTENTS

FOREWORD

This might seem strange, but once when I was a teenager my father told me I shouldn't read so much. Well, actually what he said was I shouldn't read so much science fiction. There were, he claimed, other forms of literature. But for me, disappearing into the couch with my Monkees and Beatles records and my stack of the latest paperback gems from Asimov, Clarke, Ursula leGuin, Stanislaw Lem, Spider Robinson and dozens of others, there were whole universes to explore, including unknown planets, alien creatures and civilizations, future societies, and alternate pasts. Maybe some of it was deficient in character and dialog and those other qualities that supposedly existed in real literature. But damn, it was fun and made me think and dream. It also provided a sort of world view for me and a small community of friends who were hooked on space and SF (we did not call it *sci fi*) and futurism. It may sound corny, but science fiction really was a major source of inspiration for me both to seek a career in space science and to imagine a better future for humanity.

The stuff we liked best was "hard" science fiction, written by people who knew some science (including social science) and wanted to explore stories that might manifest within universes constrained by physical reality as we understand, or may misunderstand it. They often let the story be driven by puzzles or constraints raised by science. There's a saying among nerds who advise Hollywood that "the story always comes first," meaning that if you want the writer or director to incorporate some cool or realistic science you should understand that this is always the lowest priority. This may be a useful rule for not getting thrown out of a studio, but it's not the way to make good science fiction. Such productions often just half-assedly accommodate some sciencey jargon as an afterthought to achieve a veneer of authenticity. But real science fiction of the kind I fell in love with frequently builds the story around some scientific or philosophical puzzle, using some out-there speculation or plausible invention as a device to shape the rest. The science provides the nucleus of the story.

In the 1960's and 1970's, hard SF writers consumed and processed the results of the earliest space flights and helped us all figure out their meaning. They took what was happening and extrapolated it into the future, helping us see where we might be going. And in turn the SF writers inspired new generations of space explorers, and fed them ideas. There's a fruitful feedback between science and science fiction. I've experienced this first-hand, feeding off the SF literature but also helping some writers out with speculative ideas about possible alien life. Astrobiology is especially fertile in this regard, as it is inherently extrapolative, and is constantly in need of fresh thinking and playful assaults on its many tentative consensus assumptions. In turn, new ideas and discoveries from astrobiology provide a nutrient flux for the metabolism of science fiction. There's a definite symbiosis between the communities (and some actual overlap). This feedback gets short-circuited when, as in the collection of stories you are now reading, the scientist and the story writer are one and the same.

The book you are holding contains the handiwork of a creative group of scientists who are uniquely placed to continue this feedback into our new world of exoplanets, extremophiles, private space programs, and the swirl of utopian and dystopian future visions arising from the chaos of our current politics. Astrobiology is a relatively young beast–forged by endosymbiosis, a merging of once separate disciplines feeding off of one another, joining to create a new type of creature with skills neither possessed before. Out of this has emerged a cadre of young scientists with unsurpassed skills at communication across boundaries and wide-ranging imaginations. The Blue Marble Space Institute of Science is a nexus of bright, (mostly) young, ambitious, idealistic, entrepreneurial, optimistic and creative scientists who are not just willing but downright eager to violate disciplinary expectations. It's the place you would expect to hear the answer, "No good reason," to the question, "Why shouldn't a research institute publish a book of fiction written by scientists?"

This book contains eleven expansive stories written in a wide range of voices and styles, each challenging and entertaining in its own way. To me, reading it felt like a guilty pleasure. Can it really be this much fun to immerse in such thought provoking scenarios, ideas, and possible futures? Opening it reminded me of the feeling I used to get when a new issue of *Analog Science Fiction and Fact* would show up in my suburban mailbox, with its mix of fiction and speculative science essays. Then, it wasn't just about the stories but also a connection with a certain culture and its techno-utopian mindset. We believed that space and technology would move hand in hand with social progress toward an enlightened multi-planet human future which would be both more equitable and more fun. Inspired by SF and the space colony designs of Eugene O'Neil, my high school friends and I assumed that parts of our 21st century adulthood would be spent off world and that this expansion would be part and parcel of greener Earth management.

But then 2001 came and went. We still don't have a moon base or human missions to Jupiter and beyond the infinite (let alone paranoid computers, though we're getting there…). And while I don't buy prophecies of doom, one must admit we haven't exactly turned the corner on our gravest environmental and social challenges. Sometimes in recent years I have felt cynicism gnawing at the edges of my adolescent utopian space dreams. I still believe it's our destiny to leave our earthly cradle, explore and live widely, and in so doing learn new ways to treasure our home planet. But I have not always been able to emotionally connect the dots between our current halting progress and those dreams, which seem to recede into the future beyond my own likely demise. Not only that but I see elements of those dreams being repackaged to serve visions that strike me as elitist, escapist, or non-inclusive in ways that repel me.

So, reading these stories was a good experience for me. And I don't just mean that they are fun to read, though that they are. I liked being immersed in the allegorical worlds of the Blue Marble Space Institute of Science because, in these varied playful ways, they are wrestling with real problems. They aren't just obsessed with space and science. They also seem to care immensely about helping to create a just, sustainable and equitable future. They remind me of my better self: uncynical, open minded, in love with the universe and with knowledge and exploration of it, idealistic and seeking new solutions. Each of the stories in this collection is a short journey that pulls you out of your current time and then returns you changed in some way. I hope you enjoy them as much as I did.

David Grinspoon
Washington, D.C.
July 2017

TWO LEAGUES OF DARKNESS

SHAELYN SILVERMAN

*A*part from the Earth-like geysers jetting out into space, the lunar surface in the photo looked completely foreign under the jet-black sky. The image was captured by NASA's Cassini-Huygens spacecraft during a flyby of Enceladus in 2005—some 52 years earlier—rendering the moon the popular subject of many imaginative pieces of science fiction. Particularly enthralled by the implications of a great subsurface ocean in this picture was 32-year-old oceanographer Justin Pierce, who had reveled in the ocean's mystery ever since he was a young boy. To many, the ocean was an entirely separate world, filled with uncharted wonders among its vast, lightless depths. However, to Justin, the terrestrial sea had always felt like more of a home than any stable landmass. From learning to swim before he could walk, to developing into a world-class swimmer, to eventually translating his passion into a career with NOAA (the National Oceanic and Atmospheric Administration), Justin had spent the majority of his life in the water. After earning his doctorate in marine biology at Duke University, he had spent the last four years researching oceanic eddies in the North Atlantic ocean at the

NOAA Florida Keys National Marine Sanctuary.

With one last glance at the famous photograph of Enceladus hanging in his office, Justin switched off the lights and headed down the hall, out the building to prepare for his morning dive. The walk to the edge of the dock where Justin's Bayliner *Sundancer* dive boat was parked was approximately 200 yards, and in the distance he recognized his colleague leaning over the boat.

"José," he excitedly called out.

"Justin, my man." José pushed himself off the boat's stern and greeted Justin with their familiar handshake. Now colleagues at NOAA, the two had first met during their graduate school years at Duke and quickly became good friends, sharing long hours of sleepless nights writing their dissertations interspersed with an equal number of nights chasing uninterested women at the local bars.

"It's good to see you back in one piece. How was your trip?"

"Oh, you know. Just the usual black hole in the middle of the ocean deciding to change course and head straight for us, forcing us to immediately evacuate in an orderly panic. I swear there's never any adrenaline rush associated with this job anymore," José laughed. He had just returned from a two week long research expedition studying a baroclinic mesoscale eddy in the Agulhas Current that had been intensifying over the last two months.

Justin chuckled. José never missed an opportunity to crack a joke, and there never seemed to be a dull moment when Justin was around him.

In conjunction with Justin's lifelong love for the sea, he possessed an equal fascination with space exploration, as the world was amidst an era of technological revolution, and rapid advancements were being made every few years. For the most part, the nations were cooperating peacefully; however one country in particular, Sokovia, had risen up and become a malicious competitor in the space race. Sokovia viewed the planets and moons in the Solar System as resources to exploit, neglecting the planetary protection laws revered by the rest of the world.

Justin shook his head in frustration at this thought as he packed his bag for the day, preparing to return home. He remained deep in thought for most of the journey to his car until he suddenly had the unnerving realization that the parking lot was unusually empty and quiet. Wondering where everyone had gone, he quickened his pace to his car.

As he unlocked his car, he perceived the silencing of an engine as a car rolled to a stop directly behind him. He immediately felt a sense of panic and spun around. Two unfamiliar men with sunglasses and baseball caps sat in a black Rolls-Royce that was now three feet from Justin, giving the impression of imminent danger.

"Justin," one of the men quickly asserted before Justin could run. "Don't be alarmed—we have a message for you." He pulled out a sealed envelope devoid of writing and handed it to Justin. "Wait until you get home to read this, and don't tell anyone" the man stated. With that, the car sped off as quickly as it had come.

Justin stared in disbelief at the envelope in his hand

for several minutes. *What had just transpired?* On his ride home, the scenery blurred by as unceasing questions circulated through his mind. *What possible message could be contained inside the lines of the letter? Who were these men?* And more importantly, *why was he—an ordinary civilian –handed this letter?* Pulling into his driveway, he could not shake the uneasy feeling that someone was watching him. He surveyed his front yard for a minute before slowly approaching his front door and cautiously entering his house. After convincing himself that he was alone, Justin removed the envelope from the pocket lining the inside of his jacket and carefully examined it. The envelope did not appear to contain any biological or technological threat, so he carefully tore it open. Printed across the top of the letter were three words that accelerated Justin's pulse: NATIONAL SECURITY AGENCY. After a deep breath, he read the letter:

Dear Mr. Pierce,

On behalf of the Director, National Security Agency/Chief, Central Security Service (NSA/CSS), you are hereby ordered into service of the United States Government. The contents of this mission cannot be disclosed in writing; your presence alone is therefore required at 0700 hours on the 19th of August, 2057 at the intersection of United and White Street to receive further details.

STEVE NEWMAN, Ph.D.
Counter Intelligence & SIGINT
National Security Agency

The world around Justin seemed to stand still yet simultaneously spin in a whirlwind of chaos. Nausea swept over him, and he could no longer stand upright, as the ground upon which he was walking suddenly became foreign surface unsupportive of his weight. Previously unanswered questions resurfaced. *Was this real? What did the NSA want with him?* He looked at his watch. *Jesus.* He had 11 hours until he would be forced to succumb to this fate, whatever it may be. He began to pace through his house and eventually realized he was in the kitchen. Having no appetite, he found his way to his bed, but all efforts to sleep were futile. Time flowed but Justin was oblivious to everything except for a fixed spot on his ceiling, which seemed to occupy his attention for the majority of the night.

The digital clock in Justin's car read 6:53 when Justin pulled into the parking lot of a small coffee shop. The world, oblivious to his presence, was just beginning to wake up. He cut his engine and scanned the surroundings for several minutes, but nobody stood out as someone who would be part of the NSA. Frankly, he didn't even know who he was supposed to be looking for. *Will they be wearing a suit with sunglasses, or will they inconspicuously blend with the rest of the crowd?* His question was soon answered when there was a tap on his window. A woman dressed in a white t-shirt, blue jeans and sunglasses leaned toward his window as Justin rolled it down.

"Dr. Pierce," she flashed a golden SPECIAL AGENT badge, "please unlock your car".

Justin had the uneasy feeling that she must have studied him extensively by the way she immediately recognized him. Yet he felt strangely comforted by her pleasant demeanor, and subsequently unlocked his door. Without hesitation, she climbed into the passenger seat and commanded him to the Key West US Coast Guard Sector.

"Why –" Justin began.

"I'll tell you everything in a minute. Just start driving." She retrieved a black gadget with an antenna, fitted it into a 12-volt adapter, and plugged the contraption into the car's outlet as Justin pulled out of the parking lot. She then confiscated Justin's phone and placed it in a small black pouch. "Do you have any other devices that could be GPS-tracked?"

Justin mentally enumerated all the objects in his possession before confirming that he did not.

"Good. I just inserted a GPS jammer into your car and put your phone in an anti-tracking bag. What you are becoming involved in is a current priority for national security, and cannot be known by the public. I'm Claire, by the way—NSA special agent. I know you must be very confused right now, but just trust me when I say that some very classified information has fallen into our hands, and we need your help to investigate it. You'll find out everything when we get to the Coast Guard office."

Questions he was sure Claire would not answer flooded his mind until he finally settled on one he felt was harmless. "Why are we going to the Coast Guard? Doesn't the NSA have its own office?"

"Not in the Florida Keys," Claire explained. "However,

given the gravity of the situation, four of us from the Miami division were sent out here to meet with you."

Six minutes later, Justin's car pulled into the Coast Guard parking lot, and Claire whisked him up to an office on the third floor, where he met two other men and a woman, congregating around a small transmitter on top of a conference table.

One of the men spoke first. "Dr. Pierce, thank you for joining us. I'm sorry for all the trouble we have put you through over the last 24 hours, but in a minute you'll understand why this meeting had to be completely confidential. My name is Dr. Schroder—but please, call me David. I'm the PI of the MARINE (Mission to Analyze, Research and Investigate Enceladus) team. We operate under the Discovery Program at NASA's Marshall Spaceflight Center."

The other woman, who worked on the MARINE team with David introduced herself as Maria; the final member in the room was a tall, muscular brunette man named Mark, a CIA special agent.

"In 2037," David began, "after *ELF*—the Enceladus Life Finder—was finally funded, it was sent to Enceladus to assess the moon's habitability based on biological indicators in its plumes. Given the primitive rocket technology two decades ago, *ELF* had to rely on Jupiter to perform a gravitational assist, and arrived in 2044." This information was not new to Justin; *ELF*'s launch and arrival had been heavily advertised that year. Justin was 12 years old at the time, and had been so electrified by the worldwide hype of the mission that he spent the next week launching model rockets using his own potassium nitrate-based rocket fuel.

David continued, "The orbiter carried extremely advanced mass spectrometers with high resolution and sensitivity—far more advanced than those sent to Europa—developed specifically for the mission. It collected data for the next decade, and just before it was decommissioned, it detected a very peculiar signal. However, when it sent back the spectrum, the transmission was intercepted by Sokovia, and they kept the results to themselves. We were immediately made aware of this, and spent the next six months attempting to hack their servers and retrieve the information.

"During this time, the *Atlantis* mission was developing, and we decided to proceed with it according to schedule," David recounted while Justin reflected upon this space mission as well, distinctly remembering that at the time of this launch in December of 2054, his heart was getting broken by his then-girlfriend of two years.

"*Atlantis*' mission was to drill into the crust of Enceladus at the South Pole and sample the water for more clues as to whether life could exist there. The flight took three years, and during the second year, we finally managed to retrieve the spectrum from Sokovia. What was discovered was... well, shocking, to say the least. You might want to sit down for this."

Justin took a seat at the conference table and leaned in. All eyes were on David, and the room was filled with an anxious silence.

"I want to preface by saying that the results were extensively scrutinized, and honestly, I didn't believe them at first. You're never going to believe this discovery, but TMAO was detected in the ocean."

A heavy silence enveloped the room.

David continued. "I'm sure you're quite familiar with this compound–"

"Trimethylamine *N*-oxide," Justin interjected without thinking. "But, that's impossible. It's an osmolyte found only in saltwater marine life. That would mean…"

"Yes, Justin. We have confirmed life on Enceladus. And not just molecular organisms, as we previously imagined. There is large, aquatic marine life living in the ocean of Enceladus." He allowed Justin to absorb this.

Justin was quiet, but his mind was racing. *What kind of macroscopic life could be adapted to a subsurface, alkaline ocean of extreme salinity?* His thorough knowledge of Earth-based marine organisms hindered his imagination for the physiology of aquatic life outside of this planet. "So what did the *Atlantis* team find?" Justin suddenly became aware that he was visibly leaning over the conference table toward David, and quickly receded back into his seat.

"That's where the… uh," David looked around the room at the others, who each gave an imperceptible nod, "covertness of this mission comes into play. We didn't want to alarm the public, but we lost contact with the *Atlantis* crew five months ago. This was the last transmission that came through." David pressed a button on the transmitter centered on the conference table.

The sound of human speech crackled to life on the device, but the words were incomprehensible. David adjusted the bandwidth and played with the fine-tuning controls until the speaker's words became coherent.

"...now our 18th day on Enceladus. Yesterday we finished drilling the hole. It measures 10 meters in diameter. Should be big enough for our sampling purposes. So far, we still haven't seen any obvious signs of life, but we haven't gathered any oceanic samples yet either. We'll know more in about a week. Our habitats are holding up well, and we have plenty of resources to get us through the next six months. All in all, not bad for living on a giant ball of ice. Plus, the triple layer TMG's on our suits keep us pretty nice and toasty."

The signal vanished for a few seconds, then returned.

"...definitely something weird going on here. Some kind of," the voice paused for a painful second, "energy, beyond anything we have on Earth. We –"

"Hey, Lane, come take a look at this," another voice shouted.

"Not now, Joe, I'm giving my daily newscast. Just let me have my 60 seconds of fame, will ya?" The owner of the voice was apparently named Lane.

"Dude, I really think you should get over here, now. There's something in the water. Looks like blue, sparkling light. Wait... it's disappearing, hurry."

The unmistakable sound of a headset being dropped was apparent, and the hurried sound of footsteps quickly trailed away. In the distance, at a barely audible tone, Joe's voice could be heard. "See that? What do you think it is?"

Lane spoke, "Oh my god, that's a sure sign of biolumi-nescence. Looks like those might be dinoflagellates. Wow, do you realize what this means? Sokovia's findings are con-firmed. This is first-hand evidence that there is life in this ocean, Joe. There really is life on this damn Siberian moon." He cried, "Let's get the others."

There were shouts, followed by the slamming of doors. Suddenly, there were too many footsteps to count. Voices began chattering excitedly, and none could be individually made out until one woman commanded everyone's atten-tion. "Guys, GUYS. Dinoflagellates are known to use bio-luminescence as a defense mechanism. I think we need to be cautious and get away from this hole—we don't know what's down there."

"You're right Mary, everyone step back."

"I think I just saw something move in the water."

"What was it Anton?"

"I am not sure—but it was big."

"Oh shit, I just saw it too."

"What is that? It looks like a giant black mass with ten-tacles."

"It seems to be agitated by our floodlights."

"Turn off all of the lights. Helmet lights. Floodlights. Habitat lights."

"Forget it, everyone RUN."

The chaos that ensued was unsettling, and Justin felt a numb detachment from the recording as his mind was taken back to middle school when he often was forced to suffer through horror movies that his friends insisted upon watching while he would close his eyes and try desperately to block out the sounds.

Cries for help wailed out. "It's got me." Then, a splash, cutting off the screams of one individual.

"That was Vladimir." Another splash.

And one by one, screams were mercilessly drowned out until a ghostly silence penetrated the transmission. David quickly turned the receiver off.

For a long time, nobody said a word. It felt almost disrespectful to break the silence, as if doing so would fail to honor the lives lost. Finally, after several minutes, Mark spoke. "As you can see, we couldn't exactly share this with the public, so we have kept this in secrecy for the last five months. But did you catch Lane's comment about the energy on Enceladus?"

Justin nodded, and Mark continued, "We have decided to send another covert mission to Enceladus to gain more insight into this mysterious moon. This time, the spacecraft will contain a submarine that will be equipped with enough supplies to last a year. It will be a crewed vessel, and its mission will be to descend into the depths of Enceladus' ocean and gather data on the life there, as well as the energy source Lane referenced. We have collaborated with Roscosmos and have carefully selected a crew of the six most qualified experts whom we believe can carry out this mission. Justin," he paused, "given your oceanography expertise, you have been chosen as a member of this team."

Justin stared in disbelief for what seemed like a few eternal moments, as he allowed the information to sink in.

Weeks contracted to days, and before he knew it, Justin found himself at Cape Canaveral, looking up at *Cronus*—the spacecraft that was to be his home for the next 3 years. He smiled at the discrete metaphor; *Cronus*, the leader of the Titans in ancient Greek mythology, was father to Poseidon, god of the sea. Thus it was only fitting that *Cronus* would be transporting the crew to the distant, alien ocean. He reflected on the past month. It seemed like an eternity ago when he was ripped out of the comfortable routine of his life. He still wasn't sure that he fully comprehended the magnitude of this mission and frankly, he couldn't fathom what to expect, despite having been forced to sit through copious training and debriefing sessions. The most difficult part of this experience had been attempting to tell José that he was going to suddenly disappear for years, as he was unable to give away any concrete detail about the mission. Deep sadness overwhelmed him at the thought that he might never see his best friend again.

His thoughts were quickly interrupted as he was introduced to a few members of the crew—Anastasia Petrov, the medical specialist of the crew, had the monotonous task of monitoring the crew's health daily over entire duration of the trip while they slept. She was a petite, blonde woman with a round, young face and bright blue eyes; but one handshake quickly revealed that her dainty demeanor belied her incredible vigor. Justin was suddenly unsettled by the idea that this woman would be sticking needles in him for the next three years.

Nikolai approached Justin next. "Dr. Pierce, my name is Nik Aleyev. Systems engineer." Nik was several inches shorter than Justin, and judging by his round glasses and frequent sideways glances, Justin could tell that he was one of those brilliant engineers whose intelligence was obvious, but often had a difficult time manifesting itself through his reserved nature.

"And you must be Dr. Romanovsky," Justin turned to the tall, athletically-built man with short black hair who was walking toward him. "Please, call me Alex," the telecommunication engineer said with a pronounced Russian accent. "Follow me, I show you inside." Alex led Justin through the hatch and into the heart of *Cronus*, pointing out all the main facilities along the way. As they toured, Alex elucidated the mission in further detail. As far as the public was concerned, the mission's primary purpose was to "explore Enceladus for further indications of life," but there was no public mention of *Atlantis*' fate. The two paused in front of the ship's laboratory, and with a keypad entry of a 4-digit code, Alex enabled the sliding glass doors to open. A relatively young woman with long, brunette hair was busy at a lab bench and did not hear the two enter. "Rachel," Alex called out to her.

Visibly startled, she set her glassware down and quickly walked over to shake Justin's hand. "Hello," she cleared her throat, "I'm Dr. Rachel Scott." Justin suddenly realized from the crew's biographies that he was in the presence of the world-renowned geomicrobiologist who actively studied serpentinization—the transformation of rock into certain minerals under conditions of heat and pressure—and its implications for deep-sea life.

From around the corner, a tall woman approached whom Justin immediately recognized as Commander Andie Layne—navy seal and veteran of four spaceflights. Her short, dark auburn hair bobbed quickly, matching her hurried pace. "Dr. Pierce, welcome aboard. Alright boys, Dr. Scott, we have liftoff in 30 minutes. I suggest you get yourselves to the crew compartment now." Her piercing green eyes were intimidating, and Justin felt compelled to nod at the floor in response. She took off as quickly as she had come, moving with a swift grace that manifested her confidence. Alex suddenly broke his concentration as he laughed, "Oh no, my friend, you are rock compared to Commander Layne. She will not look at you like that. Come now, we go to crew compartment." Justin's neck immediately burned from humiliation at what had just transpired. He attempted to indiscreetly play it off but was unsuccessful, and relegated himself to silently following Alex through the ship's halls.

The compartment was significantly more spacious than Justin had anticipated. He was given no task in the process of takeoff, so instead he strapped himself in and absorbed the excitement. Commander Layne flipped a switch that illuminated *Cronus'* dashboard.

Layne: The clock has started.
MCC: Roger, *Cronus*. Thrust looks good on all five engines.
Layne: Looking good in here too.
MCC: Five minutes and *Cronus* is GO.
Layne: Roger.
MCC: Stand by for Mode V capability.
Layne: Mode V capability, and we have ignition.
MCC: Four minutes and *Cronus* is GO.
Layne: We have inboard cut-off.
MCC: Inboard on time. Houston, you are GO for staging.
Layne: Three minutes and *Cronus* is GO.
MCC: Cutoff will be at 14 plus 36, 14 plus 36.
Layne: Roger, 14 plus 36.

Justin's mind, however, was elsewhere. He was contemplating all the luxuries from his once comfortable life that he would be leaving behind—a warm bed, an immobile toilet, delicious food—things he had always taken for granted and already missed.

MCC: …eight…seven…six…five…four…three… two…one. And we have liftoff.

With an intense surge of energy followed by a great vibration, *Cronus*' engines rumbled to life. Justin's attention quickly shifted to the window, and he watched the world quickly shrink away beneath them as they accelerated upward. Pressure intensified as the thrust increased, and for several minutes he embraced the helplessness of man against the physical forces of nature. Before long, the shuttle was soaring over Africa, and Justin became aware of the unparalleled perspective of seeing the world from above—an experience shared by only a fraction of humanity. The city lights around the globe were striking against the darkness of the land, yet were quickly condensing into tiny points of light, causing the awareness of human insignificance to spread over Justin that was both sobering and breathtaking. This feeling was tacit among the crew, who remained silent for several minutes while *Cronus* propelled them across the night sky. The first rays of sunlight began to stretch over the opposite side of Earth, and soon the rest of the sun lifted up in a brilliant sunrise. As *Cronus* rocketed away from the planet, the edges of Earth soon became visible, and within another minute, Earth was no more than a round, blue marble illuminated against the black infinity that stretched before them.

After an hour, Commander Layne's voice came over the intercom. "Good evening MARINE team, this is your captain speaking. We are now reaching an altitude of 45,000 kilometers, currently en route to Jupiter. Using a gravitational assist from Jupiter, we will then slingshot past Saturn to our final destination: Enceladus.

"I want to personally thank each and every one of you for joining me on this mission. It will not be easy, and we fully acknowledge the extreme dangers associated with this undertaking, but we are the pioneers of a new era of discovery, and our work is directly important to every individual on planet Earth. So be proud of yourselves for braving the unknown and accepting this mission.

"Now, to those of you whose responsibilities begin on Enceladus, please report to the health unit where Dr. Petrov will assist you. That includes Dr. Pierce and Dr. Scott. I have nothing further for now. Thank you."

Justin looked across at Rachel, whose eyes had lifted from the ceiling at only brief intervals throughout the lift-off. She was visibly uncomfortable with flying, but attempted to appear calm as she met Justin at the entrance of the crew compartment. "Hey," Justin squeezed her shoulders, "humans have launched rockets into space for exactly a century now. We've had a lot of time to perfect this—we're going to be fine."

Rachel nodded but did not seem any more reassured. As the two made their way to the health unit, they briefly shared their history. Rachel was a professor at MIT, working on an Origins of Life project in the Summons lab in collaboration with the NASA Astrobiology Institute and Simons Collaboration on Origins of Life (SCOL). Her undergraduate degree in Molecular, Cell and Systems Biology from Oxford and graduate degree in Biochemistry from Harvard far surmounted any qualified professional he knew in the field, and from their brief conversation, her profound intelligence was obvious. In turn, Justin shared about his academic career and work at NOAA. Through their short walk across the shuttle, Rachel's nerves became more agitated and she quickly interrupted him. "I'm sorry, spaceflight is so foreign to me. And on top of that, I have a fear of flying on normal airplanes."

"Hey—don't apologize. If, no, *when* we make it to Enceladus, I'll buy you a drink." Justin promised. "It's normal–"

"Rachel, Justin," Ana interrupted their conversation, "let's get you guys to bed." Hesitant to leave Rachel but obligated to obey orders, Justin followed Ana to the health monitors for some blood work. When he returned, Rachel was staring idly at the walls, awaiting her turn. She smiled at him as he passed, and subsequently followed Ana over for her examination.

Justin began to inspect the pressurized chamber—the habitat in which he would reside for the next three years in a cryogenic sleep. The bed—if it could even be called that—was a cold, hard, uninviting table in the hole of the machine, covered by a glass lid that left the subject completely exposed to any passerby. *The MARINE team is going to be very close by the end of this trip*, he thought.

"Your vitals look good, Dr. Pierce," Ana announced as she made her way over to Justin. For a small woman, she could really fly around the room. "Please get into your bed. I'm going to hook you up."

Justin's suspicions were confirmed when he lay down; the habitat was less than comfortable. Luckily, he would only be conscious of this fact for a brief period of time. No sooner had he settled when Ana began attaching sensors to his body, darting back and forth between Justin and Rachel so that she could synchronize the shutdown of their vitals. In them, Ana inserted intravenous tubes for total parenteral nutrition, and a catheter for handling waste. Finally, she attached electrical muscle stimulation pads on Justin's arms and legs to induce muscle contractions during their hibernation period, counteracting muscle atrophy.

"Lowering the shields," Ana declared when she had finished hooking her patients up to the system.

Suddenly, Rachel called out, "Justin—when we make it to Enceladus, I'll take you up on that drink offer."

Justin smiled, and Rachel's voice was the last sound he remembered before the shield lowered, his eyes closed, and a calming icy gas was blasted into the chamber. His breathing dramatically slowed, and as far as he was concerned, for the next three years, the universe was quiet.

THE MARTIAN
AIR CRISIS

JACOB HAQQ-MISRA

"*C*oming to bed?"
"I have to sell."
"Everything?"
"Tomorrow. When the markets open."

"Our family will make it."

"I know. But only if we sell." Muffled sirens permeated the air, and a waft of diesel fell through a crack in the window. The hazy sky stood cloudless and starless as the cityscape faded into twilight.

"Why did they have to go to Mars, anyway?"

"To beat the Chinese."

"Too soon, though."

"Six lifetimes' worth of air debt per colonist. A broker's dream."

"More like a nightmare."

"Everyone thought they'd keep up their premiums. No one saw this coming."

"Congress."

"Eliminated all oxygen subsidies, twenty years early. Industry can't cope this fast."

"Those poor people..."

"Don't give me that guilt trip. We have our own mortgage to worry about, the lake house with your sister's studio, the bill for my cousin's rehab, and the homes for both our folks—and school only costs more as the kids grow. We're sitting on a pile of air and losing money every minute."

"So what happens next?"

"We sell and live out our lives. Get back to trading energy securities, and forget about the fortune we lost on Mars."

The screech of tires punctuated tension in the room as a chorus of horns echoed anger from the accident outside. "What will happen to the colonists?"

The long pause spoke to the truth they both knew. "It doesn't matter. The colonists all defaulted on their loans, so the bubble has burst. Got to get out while we can."

Their eyes drifted to the window and strained at the sky, but Mars was nowhere to be seen. Each breathed a deep sigh of terrestrial air and reveled in the familiar scent of urban night.

"We should get some sleep."

"I've got too much on my mind."

"You said to forget about Mars."

"Trust me, Mars is the least of our problems."

NEXT
NEXT-GENERATION
SEQUENCING

SIMON GONZALEZ

A psychiatrist and a molecular biologist plopped their butts down on the diner's red glitter-vinyl cushioned booths. The brisk afternoon called for coffee, though not at the lukewarm temperature at which the robo-waiter served.

"*Heeey* Claudia, thanks again for getting back to me so quickly. And really, it was great of you to even help out in the first place. This patient of mine is hopeless. He still can't seem to move past his 'alien abduction,'" Allen said while making air quotes with his fingers (on one hand only, the other hand was wrapped around the coffee mug, a desperate attempt at insulation).

"And here I was just telling my husband how it almost feels like there's no use for biologists anymore, since the singularity ban and all," Claudia said with clear enunciation. She hid her annoyance at the air quotes well enough.

"Well, if your biotech company hadn't revealed the plan for the 'perfect' human, it wouldn't've been so bad. The economy needs sick people to buy fixes." He knew he had to walk back his accusatory tone. "At least we both still have jobs, though."

The unintentional slight reminded her that the past, after all this time, still had the power to take small bites out of her composure at any moment. It was unnerving. Sensing this, Allen grabbed the shared coffee pot and refilled her mug.

"And I wouldn't normally ask anybody to investigate a crazy claim like this, but if this guy, this patient of mine, is able to get some closure, it means I can get him permanently off my to-do list. So, what's the deal? Were you able find out if there's a secret message in his DNA, like *they*, the *aliens*, told him was the case? If so, all he has to do is recite it and they'll stop coming after him."

"It wasn't any bother at all, really. The gene analysis app on my phone let me analyze his spit sample with ease. Sorry I didn't reply to your e-mails sooner—grants and stuff."

"Got to pay that outrageous Austin rent, am I right?" Allen thought about his New New Braunfels mortgage while he said this.

"Don't remind me. If aliens were actually abducting people at least the housing market would take a hit. But anyway, maybe with this gene scan result he can rest easy knowing there aren't any little green people messing with his DNA anywhere," she said.

"Finally, an expert opinion he might listen to. I'm tired of hearing this guy go on and on about getting probed. What's even more nuts is the thought that anybody'd want to. So, everything checked out?"

"Well, yes… and no. Predictably, his DNA profile shows he has a strong probability of suffering from—no surprise here, paranoid schizophrenia. And there is no 'special DNA' sequence with any kind of encoded information. But there is *something else*." She let a smile steal the corner of her mouth.

"Go on…"

"Well see, there's this old idea about a hidden biosphere—the shadow biosphere."

"Sounds dark? I'm all ears, buddy. As long as we're not talking about shadow aliens probing my patient. Then I'm going to have to take this cold coffee to go," he said. Subconsciously, his anti-robot prejudice grew.

"Not aliens, not quite. It's an ecosystem of organisms which, some argue, we have yet to discover here on Earth. Creatures which happen to not use DNA. No evidence for this, so far, of course. Unless you count the odd behaviors of certain clays. Anyway—"

"When you guys catalog any animal or bug in biology it's based on DNA sequencing, reading the DNA. How would you find a shadow species— using your instruments—that doesn't have any DNA?" Allen imagined Claudia hunched over a lab bench, and then visualized himself, in his comfortable leather chair, notepad and pen in hand. Both thoughts tired him. This also put the caffeination of the coffee under suspicion.

"That right there is precisely the question of relevance. I'm sure you can see how it's related to what the aliens call 'special DNA'. Well, after we saw that his genome was typical as ever, I wondered—maybe the aliens weren't talking about a special sequence of DNA but actually some chemical alternative to DNA. A pseudo-DNA, not the *DeoxyriboNucleic Acid* we're used to," she stressed the first letters for emphasis like a true professor. "We'd never detect something like that because we always rely on enzymes that very specifically can only detect and read DNA."

"I see. So you'd need a special enzyme that could read this pseudo-DNA? And maybe this would support some kind of shadowy biological monster? One that's also microscopic and deadly?" Allen asked, pleased that he was following along on the Bio 101 discussion without coaching.

"Yes, I guess. The enzyme would work with any other kind of pseudo-DNA that might base pair with DNA. Get this, though, this wacky enzyme that could do something like that, interconvert between a pseudoDNA and DNA—it exists. It's called the XNA polymerase. Some completely unmodified humans engineered it from scratch over a century ago."

"XNA… 'X' like in 'X-Files'?" He was still trying to catch up on the fiftieth season.

"It can read DNA, RNA, any-NAs based on totally wild chemistries. That's what the X is for. X can be almost anything. The important thing is that it lets us sequence whatever the XNA is."

"Like the 'X-Files.'"

"No…yeah, ok, whatever *like the X-Files*." In any case, we used this XNA enzyme on your guys' cells instead of the regular DNA sequencing enzyme."

"Wait, why hasn't anyone done this before? Pseudo-DNAs littered across the planet and in our bodies would be a big deal," Allen said.

"I know, right? But remember, back then the funding was pitiful. And before people were able to get too ambitious with heavy synthetic biology, of course, there was the singularity ban," she pointed out.

"Right. My parents lived through that era and still have no clue what was going on. I guess they still think I'm a medical doctor. Whatever. Anyway, what'd you get from my patient?"

"A whole lot of pseudo-DNA T's. T's, as in one of the four DNA bases, A, T, C, or G. Only the T's. No way to write a message from the stars with just one letter, which is unfortunate for your patient's deeply held belief about extraterrestrials, I'm afraid." She caught herself wanting to make air quotes around "extraterrestrials."

"But…"

"But, we're getting a huge grant to characterize it further. My guess is the pseudo-DNA is meant to bind to DNA or RNA strands. Maybe since T's bind with A's, it hangs onto sequences that contain a lot of A's. The clear target would be messenger RNAs, which have long tails made up only of A's. If these got passed down through cells' lineages by some new mechanism, we're basically re-writing what inheritance can mean." She leaned back, letting the smile overcome her face.

"Just how big of a grant are we talking about, Claud?"

"Millions. Of pennies. But it'll do."

"Coffee's on you, then, I suppose." He buzzed the robotic waiter. "I'll have some blueberry pie, too. And some pancakes. With lab links, not the old-fashioned sausage. And everything should be warm, not hot or cold."

The android paused at the table.

He murmured, "Please."

"Right away, sir," it buzzed. Had the robo-waiter mimicked Allen's voice?

Claudia met Allen's eyes and whispered, "The truth is out there."

FIRST NIGHT

W. RICHARDSON

*A*mbassadors,
   The following statement is for you to read to the Resurrected in your charge during their First Night. If you have any concerns about your Resurrected please contact the Department.

Dear (Name of Resurrected Citizen),

We (The government and council of the state of Colorado and of these United-States) would like to offer you welcome on your First Night. Before you sits an ambassador who has been trained in the Transition Process and who will appropriately discuss information that is necessary (but not so overwhelming as to induce a state of Temporal Disorient) for you to receive on your First Night.

Select cases (those that involve a Resurrected discovered within certain locations, including but not limited to: government and council facilities, predemic apartment buildings, research laboratories, buildings of religion, or underneath playgrounds of abandoned fast-food restaurants) are to be handled exclusively by salaried employees of our department. Your case however, dear citizen, will be best handled by a valued member of the local community in which you were found. Studies have shown that transitioning in an environment similar to the one you knew before the Long Sleep reduces your risk of TD by nearly 3% (This statistic does not apply to citizens under the age of 11 as this population does not seem to be affected by Temporal Disorient.)

(—For some Resurrected, a summary of events is unnecessary as they may have been willing participants in the illegal experiments being performed by the Sycoro Bioengineering Corporation, and thus are aware of what has caused them to enter the Long Sleep. If this is the case with your Resurrected, skip forward to the section on Treatment.—)

Information of Relevance for First Night:

1. CAUSE OF THE LONG SLEEP: We are obligated to inform you that at some point in the past you were illegally subjected to an experiment that placed your body into a form of prolonged stasis. The government, while saddened by this, does not assume any responsibility for the illegal acts of private corporations. (The council had not yet formed during the initiation of these experiments and so is also not culpable). To calculate the amount of time you spent in stasis, take the year you entered the Long Sleep and subtract it from the current year: 2151.

(—Pause here and assess how the Resurrected has reacted to this. Do not be alarmed if they seem to be frozen in shock. This is an ideal state for the Resurrected to be in as it allows for you to read through the rest of this document without any interruption. If they fly into a fitful or violent rage, please contact the department. Your safety is important to us.—)

2. Upon your discovery, a trained ambassador immediately administered a clinically safe Treatment that has been in use ever since the very first Resurrected was successfully brought out of the Long Sleep. While administering treatment, the ambassador also notified City Hall of your presence so that we might be prepared to greet you and aid in your integration after the First Night.

3. No matter what year you entered the Long Sleep, many significant events will have occurred between then and now. But the First Night is not for taking a crash course in modern history. First Night is about coming to terms with and eventually seeing the great benefit of your situation. Please feel free to ask your ambassador any questions you may have but do understand that they will not always know the answer.

Thank you for your time and welcome to the present.

With Regards,
Mona Stazler
Secretary of the Colorado Department of Resurrected Citizens and Off-Planet Disappearances.

Prosper hadn't intended to sleep for one hundred and thirty years but these things, however unfortunate, do happen.

It was completely dark by the time he parked his car at the end of the dirt path. He had been hoping to complete the journey to the bunker in under an hour but nosy co-workers, traffic, and the weather were all going to make that goal impossible to reach. He got out of the car, wary of his surroundings. Instinctively, his hand reached for the can of bear spray attached to his hip, reassuring himself that it was still there. The wind was howling and the rain that had been forecasted had finally started to fall. These conditions were far from ideal but Prosper slung his bug-out-bag onto his back and began to make the nearly mile long trek to his final destination. After all, he thought to himself, there is no such thing as an ideal apocalypse.

Prosper had given a lot of thought about how the world would end; in fact, he spent most of his time thinking about it as well as how he could survive. Whenever his co-workers grated on him more than usual, oblivious to how quickly their lives could change, and how quickly they would perish in the chaos that followed, numbers and percentages would begin to flow through his head.

Smaller disasters, such as another economic crisis, could still result in anywhere between five hundred thousand and one million deaths. A pandemic on par with 1918 would likely end in at least thirty percent of the population being wiped away if the pathogen wasn't contained in time. And of course, there was always the possibility of a coronal mass ejection from the Sun or a few strategically placed nuclear bombs. Either of these had the potential to knock down the power grid and fry nearly all electronics—estimates say only ten percent of the population would survive the first year. Sometimes, when in a particular mood, Prosper would pass the time on buses or in busy places by playing a twisted little game he liked to call 'one out ten'. He would look around, find ten people, and try to determine who he felt had the best chance of surviving that first year. He couldn't play this game at work, however. He only had nine coworkers and the game was boring when the answer was so obvious.

A few years before, when he still lived with his family in his hometown, his little sister tried to summon within him some empathy for all those ignorant of the truth. Prosper would often make snide remarks, belittling the pastimes of all those around them who lived their lives as if they did not live atop a wicker man already beginning to smoke. His sister would quickly jump to their defense, imploring him to feel pity, at least once, for those that would get caught up in the coming tempest.

Miranda had always been naive, never fully aware of the true nature of the world they lived in. She had never known anything more than her small family and the seemingly safe community in which she was raised. She had never felt the sting of abandonment, having only been two years old when their father left and never returned. But Prosper knew. He knew that their town, insulated from the world by mountains and wealthy tourists, was merely a mirage, a false glimmering reflection on the surface of a lake that concealed the troubled and dark waters below. He knew society was weak, its fingernails gripping the final edges of a great cliff. His father had told him to never trust anyone completely and to always prepare for the worst, a lesson he had cemented by abandoning the people who trusted him the most. And Prosper had prepared. He took the twelve years of lessons his father had left him and prepared for the day society would fail.

Today, he admitted, was not that day.

But he had to approach it as if it were, in order to truly run an accurate drill for the duration of the next week. He had almost left his car at work and walked the thirty miles to the Bunker. Once he'd seen the weather report, however, Prosper decided that particular aspect of the drill could wait for another day. Other than that, he would need to fully commit to the scenario. There would be no returning to the surface in order to get a breath of fresh air, or to make a late night pizza run. His coworkers could laugh and bother themselves with their frivolous interests for another day. It was too late for most of them anyway.

He was nearly at his property. It was hard to see clearly, even with the flashlight in his hand, but he had made the trek through these woods so often he was confident of his course. The rain pelted at him as his boots threatened to stick in the mud but he soon found his way to his small patch of land. No buildings were visible to the eye, only trees, mud, and if one looked closely enough into the trees, what appeared to be a large pile of rocks.

Running through the now torrential rain, Prosper approached the deceptive sculpture and felt around for a familiar pattern of notches. His trained fingers made quick work of it and the hidden electronic door popped open ever so slightly, allowing him entrance into his bunker. He descended the steps, congratulating himself on his successful arrival to safety. Upon entering to the main room, he flipped a switch and was pleased to see all the lights flicker on. The generator was working.

Prosper took a moment to survey his little kingdom. A bed, a table, and a sofa chair made up the bulk of the furniture. The rest was dedicated to storage. Shelves lined the walls of the main room and of the bathroom that adjoined it. Reference books took up an entire section; his food stockpile took up four more. The bathroom was mainly medical supplies and other various hygiene necessities. A single shelf was home to eight books, gifts from Miranda. Initially Prosper had rejected the idea of wasting space on frivolous personal items but, no matter how hard he tried, he couldn't deny the possibility that he might get bored during the potential months, or years, he would spend in this shelter.

Satisfied that everything was as he last left it, he unpacked his bug-out bag and placed its contents in their respective locations. The last item, a bottle of pills, he placed on the small table; they were to be his dinner. He had received them in a package from his mother. The attached note claimed they were miraculous, containing all necessary nutritional value a person needed. Prosper was not convinced; it all sounded too good to be true. If real, there would no longer be a need to stockpile years worth of non-perishable foods. A stockpile of the pills would be all that was necessary. He was sure this sort of item would have made the news, or at least the apocalypse message boards he frequented online. But his mother was just as experienced at preparing as he was and so he'd resolved to try them for the drill. He planned to monitor himself each day. Any sign that could be attributed to malnutrition and he would immediately switch back to his rations. That was the plan.

Prosper walked to the far corner of the bunker and was surprised to feel a slight draft coming from the second entrance. This entrance was a system of two wooden trapdoors. The first was concealed by a second pile of rocks high above that, upon closer inspection, were revealed to be the walls of a dried up well; the second trapdoor lay at the bottom of this well and lead directly into the bunker. It was meant as a safety mechanism, in case the electronics were not working and he couldn't get into the shelter using the more sophisticated door. It was a point of weakness that he needed to work on, especially if there really was a draft. Air coming in from the outside meant the first trapdoor wasn't sealed properly. Frustrated, Prosper resolved to have a look in the morning. It was not safe now, during a thunderstorm.

He had used up nearly all of the inheritance he received

from his absent father having the place built. It was supposed to be top of the line but without any of the unnecessary luxury items that were becoming so popular on the bunker market these days. He had air filters and a sewage filtration system that allowed him to reclaim water from his waste. He had two generators and a rather formidable Faraday cage which contained radios, batteries, and other precious electronics. He had spent all the money he had and all the free time he could afford and that would be for nothing if he was so easily exposed to the outside world.

He sat down angrily at the table and worked to unscrew the cap on the pills his mother had sent. Popping one in his mouth he began to chew, his face scrunching up as the taste of old pennies filled his mouth. He began to calm down as he swallowed the vile thing, as he reminded himself it was extremely unlikely that anyone would discover the trap door in a single night. This is what this week is for, finding the holes in the plan and fixing them. It was not life or death—yet.

Grumbling he got up from the table and made his way over to the bed. It was still early for the rest of the world but tomorrow he had to get up and do system checks on every piece of equipment in the bunker. This, combined with returning to the surface to check for exposures would take a long time and he would need to get up early.

He laid down in the bed, silently relieved by his choice to splurge on a high end mattress, the one luxury item he allowed himself. He took a moment to listen and revel in the silence that surrounded him. This place, more than the condo he lived in surrounded by other, noisier tenants, was his true home. He had put so much effort and care into its construction and he was thrilled to finally put it to legitimate use. There would be no knocking on his door, no neighbors throwing parties, no school children trying to sell him magazines, wrapping paper, or cookies—although he didn't really mind the cookies. He was alone and he relished in it. There was nothing that compared to this feeling of solitude- he could practically convince himself that there was no one else in the world. He closed his eyes with a small contented smile on his face.

And he slept.

And he woke. Abruptly.

The noise of a knocking had him intending to surge forth from his bed, to seek out the source of the disturbance but Prosper found he could not move. His arms nor his legs would stir beneath the covers that pressed down heavily on him. He had somehow managed to wrap himself up in a cocoon over the course of the night. He marveled at how tightly he was confined. Slowly, and with great effort, he began to wiggle himself back and forth until the sheets, which felt unfamiliar and strange in his foggy mind, loosened around him. Even with more space to move Prosper found it took an extreme effort to even bring his arms up and out from under the sheets. When he finally managed to do so he became even more disturbed as he found his arms were covered in a sheen of sticky sweat that smelled strongly of peppermint. Disgruntled and slightly nauseous from the intense smell he forced himself to sit up, the sheets of the bed falling away. Dismayed, he noted his entire body was coated with the smelly sweat but the more pressing issue was the intense pain sitting up had caused him to feel in his stomach. Or perhaps that was just hunger? He tried for a moment to stand but knew almost immediately his legs would not support him. Supporting himself on the bed he reached towards a nearby shelf for a can of his favorite canned beans. Angrily he fumbled with a nearby can opener, failing miserably at the coordination required to twist the knob; his fingers felt sore, unused. He grumbled to himself. That was the last time he ever ate something that his mother recommended. How could those supplements possibly claim to supply all nutrition needed when he could barely move from weakness after a single skipped meal? Why would his mother send him something with such disappointing results? And he hated the smell of peppermint.

Feeling slightly better after this internal rant he found his fingers had lost some of their soreness and could now grip properly onto the can opener. No sooner had he took a gulp of the beans did he spit them back out, into the can, and all over the bed. Cursing loudly he continued to spit, upset over the mess but desperate to have the mushy, off-putting substance out of his mouth. It tasted nothing like the beans he usually enjoyed feasting on. Nor did the next can or the can after that. He furiously worked the can opener on a fourth, breathing becoming a labor, but he didn't even need to taste it, as the congealed mess within was off-putting enough on its own.

Desperate for something, anything, at that point he grabbed a nearby bottle of maple syrup off the wall. He gulped it down greedily, marveling at how incredibly sweet it was. Half the bottle was gone before he stopped himself. So much for proper rationing. The weakness in his muscles was slowly subsiding, so he pushed himself out of bed and attempted to stand. The effort of it had him gasping deeply, drawing in air as he reached for the light switch. This was not good. He must have had a severe reaction to the supplement and knew that the rational, responsible thing to do would be to head to the hospital. The thought alone made him bitter. He had meant to spend the day making his bunker all the more perfect, now he would have to spend the majority of it walking to his car and somehow finding the strength to drive to the nearest town. He huffed in anger as his fingers finally found the light switch and flipped it. Nothing happened. Unbelievable.

He had paid tens of thousands of dollars for his generators and none of them were working. For a moment Prosper considered crawling back to bed, pulling the cover over his head, and sleeping until all his problems went away. But he knew survival had to be something he would have to fight for, not something that would fall at his feet. Also, the idea of getting back under the peppermint-sweat soaked covers made him queasy.

Suddenly it dawned on him that if the generators had stopped working, and the lights weren't on, then he shouldn't be able to see details of the room the way that he could. There had to be a breach in the bunker. Immediately his eyes went to the second entrance. Sure enough, a bright line originated from that side of the room before dissipating a dim glow on the rest of the shelter. Damn it. Would nothing go right today? There was no point staying there for the rest of week if not a single aspect was working correctly. Prosper swallowed his pride and resolved to begin his journey to a medical center. As he headed over to the second entrance, he also resolved to look into finding lawyers that would help him sue the company that had 'helped' him build this piece of garbage.

To his horror, there wasn't just a breach, the trapdoor was ajar, and looking up the ladder that ascended the narrow well he could see the blue sky, meaning the first door was open as well. The storm must have been more violent than he could have possibly expected.

Prosper took a deep breath and relished momentarily the fresh air above him. He hadn't realized how musty the air was in the bunker, and tried not to think on whether this meant his filtration system had failed as well. Slowly, and with great effort, he began to ascend the ladder. As he neared the top of the well he paused and listened. He could hear the irregular knocking that had woken him up. Instinctively he reached down towards his waist, only to remember that his bear spray was not on him. He contemplated climbing back down to retrieve it but knew he probably would not be able to make it back up the well; he simply didn't have the energy.

He continued on, cautious as the knocking became

louder as he neared the top. At least a bear would have no chance of fitting into this well, he reassured himself. If need be, he could always take shelter in the bunker. Upon arriving at the top, he slowly pushed the door all the way open and peeked his head out, peering nervously into the woods. His eyes ached as they tried to adjust to the influx of light and the colors around him looked washed out with little detail. He relied on his ears as he pulled himself further out of the well. He noted, as he climbed out, how dry the ground felt- unusual, considering the storm the night before. The knocking had ceased—the wind didn't even stir the trees it was so silent. Off in the distance a woodpecker's work broke the silence of the forest but Prosper knew that he hadn't merely heard a bird trying to reach a worm earlier. No, the sound had been more of a…before he could recall he heard it again, coming from behind him.

Whirling around he opened his mouth to shout in fright but all sound was stopped by surprise at the vision most peculiar before him. The sculpture of rocks he'd commissioned to hide his entryway had seemingly tripled in size since last he saw it. More peculiar was that between him and this massive collection of boulders were five or six tall trees that had most certainly not been there when he'd arrived. Most peculiar of all however, was that in-between two of these new trees, a young woman, only a few years older than a girl really, sat before a large loom, illuminated by a sunbeam, and was weaving away happily in the middle of the forest. Golden hair was wrapped into excessively intricate braids and her skin seemed to shimmer with a luminescence as she worked the wooden contraption before her.

Miranda would have delighted in it, convinced a fairy had come to grant wishes or cause playful mischief. But all Prosper could think of, all he could latch onto when faced with the strange scene before him, was that his plot of land, which he had chosen for its remote location had somehow been discovered by another person within a single day.

"Enough of it. You're awake." She breathed excitedly getting up from the seat by the loom. This woman, weaving in the middle of the woods, dressed in what could only be described as iridescent robes that seemed to be slowly shifting colors, looked Prosper up and down and shook her head with a slight sense of wonder as if he were the oddity.

"Fortune. You're one of the lucky ones. Mummies are much more common than you." She beamed, stepping towards him. Prosper backed away slightly as she approached. He wasn't sure if she was having a stroke or if he was. He'd also suddenly become overtly aware of the fact that he was in nothing but underwear—underwear he wasn't even sure were his.

"To think a little old weaver like me would be charmed enough to find a Resurrected. I mean, of course I've met Resurrected before but they were all reintegrated, but you're fresh. And to think, so many people have been coming to the Stones for years and you were beneath them all along." She clapped her hands happily together in excitement; Prosper winced at the sharp sound. The weaver looked contrite and softly lowered her hands to her sides.

"I'm not following the transition very successfully. It's

the buzz in my blood making me all hazy minded, I am sorry." She smiled patiently at him. Prosper was overloaded with questions and sensations in such a way that he was unable to string together a response, not that he was really comprehending what she was saying in the first place. Her words were familiar individually but together they made very little sense to him. He was also becoming increasingly distracted by her robes which he would have sworn had been a shimmering turquoise when he first saw her but now seemed to be a light purple. Perhaps he was still asleep, still reacting to the pills his mother gave him, and was in the midst of some strange fever dream.

"You are very fuddled, aren't you?" She asked softly, a concerned look dawning over her face. "I was told not to move you, to let you wake in a familiar surrounding but I think it would have been simpler if I had resurrected you at home." She began to bite one of her fingernails as she gazed upon him, studying him further.

"What do you mean, resurrected?" Prosper found himself croaking, his throat sticky from the maple syrup but also, somehow, dry. There were certainly more pressing questions he wanted to ask her but she had said the word multiple times now and it was making him uneasy.

"Yes. From the Long Sleep." The Weaver nodded with relief at hearing him speak. Prosper stared at her blankly, feeling she had not really given him a proper explanation.

"This is private property. You need to leave." He demanded. If this was a dream then maybe banishing his spirit guide or whatever she was would cause him to wake-up.

If this was reality then he certainly didn't want this woman, who was clearly on several substances, anywhere near him, even if that meant he had to drive himself to the hospital.

He turned abruptly, determined to begin the trek to his car. Nausea stopped him before he could take a second step. Slowly he sank to the ground, the difficulty in breathing he'd experienced upon waking up was slowly returning and his stomach was beginning to cramp painfully.

"Hold on," the Weaver said urgently as she rushed away from him. Prosper could just make her out of the corner of his eye. She was walking back to her loom. He closed his eyes for a second to breathe deeply and when he opened them again the loom was gone and the Weaver was right in front of him. He started at her sudden nearness, he tried to push himself up, to create distance between them.

"Do not over exert yourself," she reprimanded him softly. "Your muscles haven't fully recovered from their atrophy." She tried to explain.

"What are you talking about?" He tried to yell at her but could only manage to rasp the words hoarsely.

"You ate something didn't you? You need to lie back down. We have to go home." She reached for him, placing a single hand over his nose. Before he could recoil away from her, Prosper felt his eyes grow suddenly heavy and his mind began to focus solely on the overwhelming scent of peppermint that filled his nostrils.

It was as if he had forgotten how to dream. Images would

burst before him and disappear almost instantaneously, failing to create narratives. Memories and old thoughts popped in and out of existence as if his brain was running a systems check, riffling through all of its stored data files. Noises came in and out of focus, just as incoherent as the visions. When he finally opened his eyes Prosper's heart ached slightly. The last image he had seen before waking was his sister's face.

Once again he had to adjust to the light around him- this time was easier though as he seemed to be in a naturally dim main room of a cabin. The very first thought that came to his mind was: Wood. The entire room was wood. Not just the walls and the floor and the ceilings but also the furniture, the shelves and cabinets, counters, strangely enough even what he assumed were the appliances. The most eye catching thing in the room was a massive, more than comically large, wood table in what Prosper believed to be the dining area. He estimated that it could easily hold twenty people and yet his and another chair were the only two seated at it. The chair he was sitting-more like lying in really- was a curiosity all its own. It looked like wood and had the texture of wood but it was cool to the touch and cushy soft in all the right places. He wondered if every piece of wood in this room felt like that. It also began to dawn on Prosper that he had no idea where he was.

"Are you fully awake? Can you move?" A voice came from beside him, causing him to jump. Prosper turned his head towards the voice, only to see the Weaver from the woods smiling at him. In that moment, everything that had happened earlier in the day rushed back. He must have passed out…no…he remembered.

"You drugged me?" He breathed in sharply, recalling how easily he had fallen asleep as as she had placed her hand, reeking of peppermint, over his nose. He realized with renewed dismay that he was once again wrapped in sheets, though not as tightly as before, and that those sheets smelled heavily of the winter fresh gum his father used to constantly chew.

"Yes, of course." The Weaver nodded matter of factly. "You were too weak to make it back here awake and the Transition encourages frequent reapplication of the sedative. Treatment works better on a sleeping body. But you should be proud of yourself for how well you're doing. Most of the cases I've read about take weeks to recover and you seemed fairly steady earlier despite only a few days of treatment."

Treatment? Oh god. Prosper felt that same sense of unease he had felt when she kept repeating the word 'resurrected', only this time the unease was more like a fully-fledged dread. He had come to the foothills to find refuge from a civilization-ending apocalypse and had managed to get himself captured by a serial killer. For a moment he cursed his isolationist instinct. If he had told his mother and sister what he was doing that week then he would have at least had hope someone might notice his absence. If he had brought his phone with him, instead of foolishly choosing to leave it behind to avoid distraction, he could have called an ambulance from the safety of his bunker and would never had met this psychotic woman. Except, he remembered, she had apparently found him already. Had he not been wrapped in that strange material upon waking up this morning? Had he not been stripped out of his clothes? He'd been so disoriented from whatever poison she was pumping into him that he hadn't given either of these odd details more than a moment of thought. For a second, Prosper felt guilt over the animosity he had felt towards his mother that morning. The pills she had given him were probably perfectly fine, it was the peppermint slime that had made him sick. He dwelled on this for a moment before his brain forced him to realize that something had been said that was very, very, not right.

"What do you mean a few days of treatment? I only arrived at the bunker last night." He said, trying to keep his voice steady, not wanting to incur the wrath of his captor before he could figure out a way of escape. She was crazy. That was certain. But the clarity with which she spoke was unnerving—she clearly believed every word she had said. Could it be possible that this substance, whatever it was, had knocked him out so deeply for so long?

Her face fell at his question, as if she had been expecting and dreading it.

"Well, we have arrived at the issue now." She said, more to herself than to Prosper. "I'm not entirely prepared for this part, to be true."

Oh here it comes, Prosper thought to himself, preparing to hear whatever strange and twisted story she was going to tell.

"I've been going to the Stones for nearly six years to do my weaving and hundreds of others have come and added rocks to the pile while on their hike. It's been a yearly tradition for students since I was a little girl. I was trying to find a rock I had placed on my seventh birthday, when I caused a whole pile of them to slide and tumble away, exposing the wood door..."

Prosper turned to her.

"Listen, lady, I don't know why your telling me these lies. That pile of stones has been there for less than a year. It's not even real stones. It's concrete sculpted and painted to look like boulders. I'm the one who had it put there." He tried to keep himself from shouting but was not very succesful.

For a second, the Weaver's eyes widened as if some great secret had finally been revealed.

"Fascinating." She whispered to herself before frowning again and looking back at Prosper.

"I see your confusion, but I'm not being false." She said quietly. "You have not been awake for a very long time. You have gone through the Long Sleep. Some people, people who carry luck in their pockets, are found fairly soon after they enter, others are not. Some are never found and some, by the time they are found, are mummies."

She was looking at him, searching his face for something but only found an angry confusion.

"Oh enough of it. I don't know why I thought I could do this on my own, I'll just have to read the Standard."

The Weaver threw her hands up in frustration before reaching into the robes of her dress and pulling out a piece of paper. Her brow was furrowed as she unfolded it and one of her braids was coming loose. She looked almost like a petulant child. Prosper couldn't tell how old she was but he would have guessed not much older than his own sister. With a final glance at Prosper, she began to read.

Prosper sat stony faced as he listened to the message being read aloud. There were several aspects that he found problematic. Firstly, he was concerned by the repetitive use of the words 'First Night'. He wasn't sure what the Weaver expected of him but he would never for a second consider participating in any ritual associated with Prima Nocta. Secondly, what were Off-Planet Disappearances and why was there a whole department for them? And only slightly more disturbing than his first two issues was the fact that, for a moment, he had believed it.

Recently purchased stockpiles that had expired seemingly over night, a custom built bunker with top of the line systems that had all failed in under 8 hours, a dry forest the night after a thunderstorm, trees where there shouldn't have been trees. All the events of this morning seemed to suggest a passage of time greater than a single day had occurred.

But it couldn't be real. There was no possible way that his body could have survived sleeping for, what was it?, one hundred and thirty five years? He wasn't an expert in biology but, as a prepper, he knew the human body needed energy to function, even while sleeping. Without a steady influx of energy, an organism would die. He could more easily explain a crazy psychotic woman in the woods going into extreme detail to plan his kidnapping. She would have to be extremely wealthy, in order to have people plant fully grown trees over-night and transport stones during the middle of a rainstorm. But still, it was easier to explain a hermetic girl with cash to burn, than it was to believe the story she was feeding him. Still, his instincts kicked in. She couldn't be older than twenty-three, so Prosper was pretty sure he could take her.

Unfortunately, he was still wrapped up in the strange sheets she had put him in and he wasn't sure how strong he was, though he did admit he felt much better than he had that morning. Perhaps the Weaver-or perhaps she was a witch-had mixed up her poison potion with one that wasn't as potent. Prosper suddenly had a plan. He would placate this mad woman, let her think he had bought into her lies. Then, the time would come when she would have to reapply the poison and in order to do that, she would have to undo his sheets. Then, he could overpower her and escape to freedom.

"You're quiet." The Weaver spoke, looking at him with concern.

"Well." He responded with his eyebrows raised. "I've just been informed that I slept my whole life away. That's a little hard to comprehend."

"You believe me?" She asked, confused. Prosper almost wanted to laugh, perhaps this woman had never won over a victim so easily.

"Why shouldn't I believe you? Why are you so surprised?" He questioned her. Perhaps he could get her to reveal the truth by accident. No, he warned himself, it would not do to aggravate her.

"I was told most Resurrected don't believe at first, that it takes time for them to accept what has happened." She shrugged. Prosper rolled his eyes.

"Why do you keep using that word? It's all a little morbid don't you think. It makes me feel like a zombie, raised from the dead." He wasn't sure why it affected him so much, but every time he heard her say "Resurrected" he would shudder internally.

The Weaver was nodding.

"Essentially yes. As long as the brain is still intact Resurrection of the rest of the body is simple but if the Chrysalis pill wasn't effective or if the effects wore off then the brain goes to mush and that's how you get Mummies." She had got up as she said this and walked over to a kitchen like area. Dried herbs and copper pots hung from the ceiling, everything else was wood.

"But if you don't like the phrase Resurrected, there are those that call themselves Travelers," she called over to him. Travelers, huh? Prosper had to admit that she was quick to improvise details, or perhaps she had an obsessively large backstory entirely memorized.

He couldn't see her very well, a wooden island was blocking her hands from view, but before long she was walking back towards the table with two steaming mugs. She set one down in front of him.

"Thanks, but I can't really move my hands." Prosper said lamely, still wrapped up in the peppermint sheet.

"That's okay, it's just as effective to inhale the steam." She explained cheerfully before breathing deeply above the mug she was holding. He decided against it, not wanting to take the chance that she had multiple ways of administering poison.

"So, these 'Travelers,' have you met many of them?" He quizzed her while pretending to breathe deeply as she watched.

"Oh, only a few." She said with a hand wave. "But that was way back when I was much younger, during my wandering days. I had only just left standard education and got myself into more trouble than I am pleased to admit." She laughed nostalgically as if remembering a time long past. Prosper frowned.

"Couldn't have been too long ago, right? I mean, you left school, what? Two…three years ago?" He watched her laugh again as he said this.

"Oh in no such way. You'd be better if you'd guessed upwards of thirty." Once again Prosper found himself rolling his eyes.

"What is that supposed to mean? When were you born?"

"2100" was the succinct yet cheerful reply that came to him. Of course she would pick such an easy year to remember, he thought to himself.

"Well, you certainly have aged well." He bowed his head to her. She tilted hers to the side in a confused response.

"What a funny thing to say. To age well." She laughed softly. "Although, I do suppose medicine has improved astronomically since you last remember."

W. RICHARDSON

"I'll say. If people in their fifties look the way you do," he responded with thinly veiled faux enthusiasm. "Tell me, what is the life expectancy around these parts anyway?" He smiled brightly at her and received a smile in return.

"Oh people have been debating that for years. But I'm not really sure. I honestly think it depends entirely on the person and the amount of risks they take in their life." She shrugged before continuing. "I do remember that last year all the Bicentenarians got together for a massive conference and celebration, but I'm not sure who the longest lived person is."

Okay. Prosper decided that this woman had definitely spent hours developing a backstory. No one could improvise this much detail without hesitation. She was an entirely different order of crazy that he had realized, although he wasn't sure what he had expected when faced with a woman who had paid close enough detail to somehow dry out the ground of the forest before he woke up. He did need to eventually figure out how she had done that.

An awkward silence had fallen. Prosper looked around for a way to break it.

"So…did you decorate your house like this to help me be less confused by my surroundings? Because, I hate to break it to you but we did have plastic and stuff in 2016." He chuckled to himself. Really though, the cabin was a bit ridiculous. Any person who wasn't from 1640 would have felt out of time.

"Is that when you're from? I'd guessed close to that based off some of the expiration dates on your stored food but I didn't know the exact year. And to answer your question, no. This house is the way that it is because that's they way I like it," the Weaver said simply. She took another long inhale of the steam from her mug. *Or because we're not in the future and so you had to build your house out of normal, not futuristic, material,* Prosper thought to himself as he looked at her intently.

"Why are you staring at me?" the Weaver said, noticing his gaze, which must have been slightly frightening. Prosper shook his head, trying to calm down and to think of topics that would keep her distracted from his true cynicism.

"Nothing, nothing. I'm just...looking to see if you have bionic laser eyes or something like that." Prosper said, grimacing at his own lame excuse. But the Weaver laughed.

"Oh, no, no. I don't have laser eyes." She giggled. Prosper nodded his head. Of course not.

"No, I don't plan on going off planet for at least five years so there's no need for all the fuss of new eyes. I just have your average strength enhancement package, which definitely came in hand when I built this place." She looked around, indicating the cabin they were sitting in.

"Wait, sorry." Prosper interrupted her quickly, not sure which point he should focus on. "You're saying you built this house yourself?"

"Yes. And all the furniture within."

He leaned in towards her, a difficult movement without the use of his arms to balance. "You're telling me that this future you live in has cured people of aging but hasn't created fully automated construction?" Her logic was slipping and Prosper, despite his desire to prevent her from becoming angry, couldn't resist poking holes in it as it slipped away.

"Just because something exists doesn't mean it's ubiquitous," the Weaver defended herself.

"But why would you build the entire thing yourself? Isn't that just a big waste of time?"

Laughter again. "You do say some strange things. How can time be wasted?" She giggled into her mug which she had finally taken a sip from.

"I only meant that you could have travelled and met people and had experiences while a machine built this house. You used your time here, building this place, when you could have been out exploring the world," Prosper clarified. The Weaver looked at him with amusement.

"I've already done those things. I traveled for nearly twenty years. I needed some alone time and so I came back here. I'll go back out again. Who knows? I'll even probably go off planet in a decade or two." She smiled.

"Okay, but to take it to this level of extreme? To build your own house? That would be like me building an entire computer from scratch." Prosper scoffed at the very idea.

"And you don't think there were people doing that in twenty-sixteen?"

"I guess there are probably a few," Prosper admitted grudgingly. "But that doesn't make it any more of a valuable pastime."

The Weaver's smile shifted into a smirk of confusion.

"Why do you get to decide what is or isn't valuable? When building this house I learnt about architecture and engineering and woodwork—obviously." She explained. "Who's to say people building computers for fun weren't also building skills that would help them create the world as it is today?"

"I highly doubt that one singular person snapping components onto a motherboard in their garage will be the defining factor in creating your world," Prosper snapped.

"I 'highly' doubt that as well, to use your expression. What great event in history was caused by one single person? What great event wasn't caused by or made up of multiple smaller, more complicated events? It is all a collaborative effort. Even if only one person's name is written down and passed along, that doesn't mean everyone else involved never existed."

The Weaver spoke with passion before gulping down the last of her tea. Or at least…Prosper had thought it was the last but when she brought down the mug he could see it was nearly full to the brim, steam pouring off, just as hot as it had been when first served.

"I'm not arguing that groups of people can't change the world. What I'm arguing is that those groups still represent a tiny portion of the population. The rest of us just sort of get carried along with the current." The Weaver's eyes widened slightly as he spoke.

"The rest of us? I'm surprised you would lump yourself into such a group." She said with candor.

"Why wouldn't I?" Prosper asked honestly. "I know my

flaws and my strengths. I knew from a very early age that I wasn't going to be able to change the world. I wasn't some scientist. So, instead, I chose to simply try and survive."

"Who said anything about Scientists?" Was her reply. "I'm a Weaver and Woodworker, not a Scientist. The society outside of that door wasn't built or saved by scientists alone. Authors wrote stories that inspired others to write more stories. Poets and Artists and Historians and Cleavers and Philosophers all helped create the culture that exists today." With each occupation her voice grew more impassioned.

"I don't know what a Cleaver is." Prosper admitted quietly but she must not have heard him as she continued with her tirade.

"Almost all people have passion or pursuits that in some way or another become a part of our culture. Why do you get to say that any individual one was worthless?" She asked him, echoing her question from earlier. For a moment, the conversation distracted Prosper from thinking about where he was and the danger he was in.

"Not worthless. Just misguided," he urged her to understand.

"They were writing their stories and singing their songs and filming their movies while simultaneously spinning towards destruction. And none of them knew. I mean, of course, we were told over and over and over again and people would sit and watch the special reports on the news and shake their head at the state of the world and then they would go to sleep, wake up and head out to enjoy whatever weird pleasure they got out of their lives without giving another thought until the next report was released." He took a deep breath, sucking in air after talking so quickly.

"But I knew, I really knew. I saw everything for what it really was and I was prepared." Prosper frowned; he realized that his entire speech had been in the past tense and he hadn't even noticed. This woman was starting to slowly drag him into her delusion.

"But that's even worse." She accused him. "You knew what was coming and yet your choice was to run and hide underground, instead of prevent what you thought could very well be the end of the species."

Now, wait a minute, Prosper thought with a grimace. Why did he feel like he needed to defend himself against this woman? It wasn't as if she had the high ground. For Pete's sake, she was trying to slowly murder him.

"What could I have possibly done? I just wanted to survive. It was already too late to fix things."

"Obviously not." She responded, waving her hands around as if somehow her cabin was proof that the world was perfect. Prosper turned away from her, anger bubbling inside. Why was he feeding into her delusion like this? Why was he letting her words get to him? He wanted to laugh bitterly at the strangeness of the situation. It wasn't enough that he was going to be murdered by a psychopath, no, no- that psychopath also had to be an extremely idealistic optimist. What kind of oxymoron?

"I'm sorry, I've upset you. We don't need to discuss this anymore. As it is, your dressing needs to be changed." She spoke as she rose from the table and began to walk towards him. Prosper froze, realizing his chance for escape had come. He had been so mentally absorbed by their strange philosophical discussion that he hadn't had time to come up with a better plan than the one he'd sketched out earlier.

"You'll have to forgive me but this will require a bit of jibbering on your part." The Weaver laughed at herself as she began to loosen the sheets.

"No worries." Prosper choked out, not caring what jibbering meant, as long as she continued to free him. It took less than fifteen seconds before he felt he could easily wrestle out of the sheets. As soon as she freed his arms he jumped up from the chair and shoved her, hard. Or at least he attempted to. Despite his best effort the Weaver had stayed entirely in place, as if made of stone. Prosper paused in confusion but, upon noticing that she too had stilled in surprise, he sprinted away and towards the door that would lead to his freedom. He burst through, out onto a porch. The cabin was on the top of a foothill that overlooked the mountains on one side and the great plains on the other. Before he could launch himself off the porch and begin sprinting down the hill he paused and stared.

The mountains were what he noticed first, more specifically the forest. The trees were so green, nothing like the red and gray husks Prosper had been used to for so long. Pine beetle had been ravaging the state's forests for years and in such high numbers that you couldn't go on a fifteen minute hike without seeing its deleterious effects. Patches of death used to cover a good portion of these mountains. But now? Not a single husk in site. The sides of the mountains were stretches of green all the way up to the alpine level. A forest ranger had once attended a Prepper meeting that Prosper used to frequent. How long had he said it would take for the forests to fully recover? Eighty years?

He whirled around to face the plains and let out a yelp of shock. For a second, he thought an entire new mountain had been erected. Upon closer inspection he saw a city, but unlike any city he had ever seen before. The buildings made the term gigantic seem inconsequential. From a distance, Prosper would have guessed the largest were half a mile thick and well over a mile high. And there were so many. And it was so sprawling. And it was so bright. "What…is that?" He breathed.

"That's Denver. That's where you'll be going tomorrow to register." The Weaver said softly, smiling in the door frame.

And suddenly, Prosper realized.

"You were telling the truth? About all of it?" he whispered.

"Yes, of course," the Weaver nodded.

Prosper shook his head. It wasn't possible. But neither was healing a forest or erecting an entire mega-city for the simple purpose of killing someone in a creative and bizarre way.

"So, you're not going to murder me?" He asked weakly, struggling to differentiate between the relief and shock he was feeling simultaneously. The Weaver laughed.

"It wasn't written in my calendar. But you will end up killing yourself if you don't come back in and let me get you the last treatment. You need to sleep." She urged.

Prosper felt airy, as if his soul could simply lean forward and leave his body. He could become a spirit. The Weaver gently grabbed his hand and began to lead him back into the cottage, through the main room and down a hallway and into a room with a bed. Prosper didn't really notice as she used a large paintbrush to coat on a gel-like substance that quickly began to absorb into his skin. He didn't make a face at the smell of peppermint and he didn't protest as she helped him onto the bed and wrapped him in yet another cocoon of sheets. She could have been talking to him or the entire process could have passed in silence. He wouldn't have noticed either way, his mind falling through holes until the peppermint lulled him to sleep.

He could hear music. Beautiful music. Thousands of chimes and bells rang out from the vast expanse of trees that surrounded him. He could hear laughter. Was that his mother? Did someone just call his name? Two figures emerged in the distance. One began to run towards him. Miranda. He tried to call her name but the bells drowned out his voice. She continued to run towards him. He wanted to go to her but his feet wouldn't move. He could see her face. Her arm outstretched to him in greeting. His eyes flew open.

The light that was streaming in was soft, early morning. At some point in the night the Weaver must have taken him out of the cocoon because he was dressed in fabric other than the sheets and there was no goop to be seen or peppermint to smell. Prosper leaned up and sat on the side of the bed. Outside his window he could just make out the edges of the great city he had seen the evening before. He wasn't sure how to react. He could only imagine how thrilled some people in his situation might be. Oh what a chance. To see the world in the future. To jump forward in time over the course of a single sleep. But he felt no hope. He felt no excitement for what lay ahead. All he wanted was to go back into his dream and be with his family again.

A sick feeling began to spread through him. He had never told his mother and sister that his bunker was finished. They would have no idea what happened to him. What if they thought he had simply abandoned them. The same way that...

"You're awake," came a voice from the hallway door. Prosper glanced up to see the Weaver. She was wearing simpler robes that day—*was this what everyone dressed like these days?* Prosper thought with slight horror. The idea of parading around in glittering gowns that shifted from one spectrum of the rainbow to another was slightly terrifying.

"It's weird. I've told you your status like that many times in the past day." She said, smiling, almost nostalgically for yesterday. "But it's time for you to leave." Her smile turned sad as she said this.

Prosper nodded and stood. Like the previous night his actions were more automatic than well thought out. He allowed her to dress him-in less noticeable clothes than hers thank goodness. He drank the strange concoction she'd handed to him for breakfast. He watched without comment as she packed up a small bag for him but hadn't really listened as she explained what to do with each item. Finally, he followed her out the door of the cabin. He let himself look one final time at the the facade of the wooden house. *How many things in there had I not understood? What technology lies within those walls that went entirely over my head?* How was he ever going to survive in this strange new world where fabrics changed color and mugs filled themselves and looms disappeared?

"…And of course I won't be able to actually go all the way to the station with you but people there are so helpful. Once you say you're a Ressur…Traveler they will know exactly what direction to point you." The Weaver was babbling on as they walked through the woods. Prosper had no idea what she was saying and he was only comprehending some of her sentences.

"…Once you get to City Hall the first thing they will do is a medical exam. Once that's over they will probably be able to tell you if you have any family waiting for you. If not, there are tons of charities…"

"Wait. What?" Prosper halted, having only just registered her words. "What do you mean they'll tell me if I have family?" He asked quickly, his heart starting to race. The Weaver looked at him wide-eyed.

"Well, it's not unlikely that if you have cousins or nieces and nephews who you've never met but are still your family. And, who knows, if you had any siblings they might still be alive. If the person was born in the 1980s there is a good chance." She smiled and began to walk again while discussing the alternate option of joining a group of Travelers. Prosper stopped listening once again. There was a chance his sister might still be alive? How old would she be now? Would she look like the Weaver or would she have chosen to age normally? The Miranda he knew would probably have embraced technology and all it had to offer. Could it be possible that he could find her?

"Well, this is where I leave you," the Weaver said, stopping suddenly by a well worn hiking path.

"You can't be serious." Prosper looked at her, wide-eyed. What exactly did she expect him to do from here on out?

"Unfortunately, I am. I'm on hermetic leave. I don't leave the forest unless there is a medical emergency. But don't worry. You'll be fine. This path leads all the way down the rest of the hill into the nearest town. Once you're there find the train station and take the next train to Denver. The ride is a bit slower than other transportation but I figure you'll be a little more familiar with trains than some of the other options. Besides, everyone at the station will want to help once they realize you're a Traveler."

Prosper stared at the path before him, unsure of how to make the next step. He turned to the strange woman by his side. "I don't know what I'm going to do in this Utopia of yours, Weaver."

She laughed happily. "Oh trust me. This is far from Utopia. We are just as you were a century ago, simply trying to move forward, to be better." She reached into the pocket of her robes and pulled something out.

"Listen. I want you to have this. Take luck for your journey and take this just in case." She handed him a small stone with strange engravings on the side.

"What is it?" Prosper asked.

"A sort of communication device. Press the markings if you can't find a group to help you at City Hall. I've linked to it so I'll know where you are and I'll have someone come get you." Sensing his hesitation she continued. "Don't be so frightened of being helped." She laughed. "These are good people that surround us." And, before Prosper could respond, she turned away from him and walked back into the deep woods. Prosper wondered if everyone he was going to meet in this time would be this eclectic and strange.

He began his way down the side of the foothills, into the valley below. As he descended he watched the sun move higher in the sky, glinting off every building in Denver. Apprehension began to fill him once again. So the Weaver hadn't tried to kill him but did that mean everyone else was as hospitable as she was? What if most people weren't so enamored with Travelers as she had been? What if people would become hostile with him? How could he defend himself against artificially upgraded people? He suddenly felt very lost and confused; the idea of heading towards a train station filled with potential threats didn't seem like a very wise decision at all.

As he walked down, he passed by three or four people. His heart would race each time but each person would simply offer a smile and continue on their hike. As they proceeded past him all he could think of was whether or not they could tell what he was. How vulnerable was he?

By the time he reached the bottom of the foothills, where the Great Plains and Rocky Mountains collided, Prosper had decided that staying out of sight was the smart thing to do for the moment.

He stopped by a small pond and looked at the stone in his hand. Part of him said to throw it in the lake. The Weaver had said she linked to it, whatever that meant, which probably also meant she knew where he was. Throwing it in the lake would prevent anyone from finding him if that's what he wanted. He could go on his merry way, not having to worry about anyone or anything and simply do whatever he wanted.

What did he want? Prosper thought for a moment. For the first time he saw himself as having a future that was totally uncertain. His whole life had been in preparation for entering that bunker and staying put. Well, he'd already done that, however accidentally. So what now?

More than anything in the world he wanted his family. If there was a chance his sister and maybe even his mother were still alive and he could get to them, to explain why he had disappeared, then he would have to take it.

That meant going to Denver, he realized with a sigh. He was going to have to register at City Hall. Still, the train station did not appeal to him. He would have to ask for directions, ask which train to take, ask which stop to get off. The more questions he asked the more attention he would draw to himself.

No. He wasn't going risk it. He would walk to Denver instead. He had always wanted to walk to or from the city.

It was only thirty miles. How hard could it be, right? Smiling, he looked one last time at the stone in his hand and the pond before him. With one last glance at the crystal clear water he turned around, slipped the stone back into his pocket, and headed to the great city to the east.

TAXON

IAN JAYMES

Someday we will travel to the stars, but biological nomenclature will never be easy.

"What's in a Name?"
Interplanetary Journal of Systematic Exobiology (2157)
24:421.

LETTER TO THE EDITOR

Dear Editor:

In a Taxonomic Note entitled "Addendum to Exobiological Taxonomy," Fitzgerald and Takahashi (*Int. J. Syst. Exo.*
2136, 3:902-912) provide numerous notes from the 7th
International Proceedings on Exobiological Taxonomy
(IPET7, 2136). Hidden among these is a change to rule
14c of the Interplanetary Code of Nomenclature of Exobiological Species. This change declares the independence
of extraterrestrial taxonomic nomenclature and indirectly
confirms the contentious "tree" system developed by Bert
and colleagues (*Astrobiology* 2125, 125:77-83).

While I applaud this nomenclatural independence

in principle, in my view this change demonstrates a lack of foresight with respect to the confusion and ambiguity which will ensue as non-Terran species and the concomitant homonyms are added to the literature by the thousands. As a member of the exobiology committee and strict proponent of the since rejected "lingua" system (Pedersen, *Xenos* 2126, 1:11-13), I can only imagine Drs. Fitzgerald, Takahashi and possibly Bert biding their time in wait to execute these changes while I was in transit to another star system. If the goal was to finally destroy the last remnants of my rational and scalable taxonomic system, then they have succeeded.

The newly established ability to transmit and receive at terabyte levels means that Eridani d and Earth will be able to communicate freely, albeit slowly. As this message transverses the ether, consider that the final insult to a reasonable taxonomic framework may leave this researcher no choice but to supersede a flawed system with his own.

Hans Pedersen
Chief Biologist, *RSV Voyager 3*
Epsilon Eridani d
(Editor's note: transmission dated March 13, 2147; Message published November 12, 2157)

"Reply to What's in a Name?"
Interplanetary Journal of Systematic Exobiology (2157) 24:611.

LETTER TO THE EDITOR

Dear Editor:

We are very sorry if we demonstrated lack of foresight with respect to nomenclatural independence and extraterrestrial life. We felt it was better to follow rules that have been used successfully for generations as opposed to the creative but flawed vision of a few scientists. Without succumbing to great detail (see IPET7) or rehashing twenty years of debate, the tree system simply adds a new taxonomic level, level "Tree", or "Arbor", above Domain that denotes planetary origin (or more specifically, a shared independent last common ancestor) while retaining a single independent code for all extraterrestrial life. In any case of doubt, this new level can be indicated using the abbreviation "a.o.e.", (*ab origine extra*). The absence of a.o.e. can then, in practice, be assumed to indicate a species from the Earth/Mars lineage. Thus a.o.e. Eridanus *Lactobacillus aggregans* indicates a species of the genus *Lactobacillus* from the Eridani tree. These rules of nomenclature are consistent with the BioCode4 standards, are just as rational as the lingua system, and are more scalable. In contrast, the lingua system proscribed a new code with its own language and rules for each new biotic system. Dr. Pedersen chose Greek for Epsilon Eridani d, but there are only so many widely understood and usable languages, and none as useful as the Latin system currently in use. If the recent report of Shahid and

Duchet (*Nature Astrobiology* 2153, 77:721-725) using the deep-space Tata-Benz very large spectral array (TB-VLSA) is correct, there may be more planets with life to discover than there are tongues of the Earth.

As for the latter concern addressed by Dr. Pedersen, we freely admit that the independence of this system allows for homonyms at taxonomic levels. However, despite the progress of BioCode in limiting new duplicates, homonyms have existed between the current taxonomic systems on Earth for centuries and science has not crumbled. Further, Recommendation 63c (IPET8, 2139) specifically discourages repeat use of common or famous names for the sake of clarity. As more "Trees" are discovered, this system can be adapted if necessary.

In closing, we would simply add that we were dismayed at the indignant suspicions of Dr. Pedersen that we in some way planned or even needed his absence to make these changes. Dr. Pedersen was chosen for the singular honor of voyaging into the stars because of his high quality of science, *not* because of his resistance to the new taxonomic system. Several scientists, and not just Dr. Pedersen, preferred the lingua system; all have since acceded to the tree system and did so at IPET7. Dr. Pedersen's solitary preference for system he largely devised in the face of countermanding scientific consensus and his willingness to use said system in counter to the IPET7 rules are of grave concern.

L. Christian Fitzgerald and Rei Takahashi
Institut Pasteur

Paris, France
December 9, 2157

"Notification of names validly published in volumes 1-5 of *EJETS*"
Interplanetary Journal of Systematic Exobiology (2163) 30:12.

LETTER TO THE EDITOR

Dear Editor:

As newly appointed director of the Eridanus Museum of Natural History, I am pleased to begin transmission to Earth the taxonomic and biological data for the numerous flora, fauna and microbiota of Eridanus that have thus far been carefully detailed and catalogued by the research members of this exploration team. Having spent the better part of five years collecting these data and secondarily considering the crisis of nomenclature upon us, I also submit the accompanying list of new taxonomic names and rules of usage that have appeared in the first five issues of the *Eridanus Journal of Exobiological Taxonomy and Systematics* (EJETS). I expect that a reply to Dr. Pedersen's previous communication is en route, but rather than wait it out or further the debate, Dr. Pedersen and I have moved to name *our* species on *our* planet *our* way. As is apparent in the accompanying list, Eridanus will use the lingua system for taxonomic nomenclature. That which we call a rose by any other name would smell as sweet. On Eridanus we shall name it as we see fit.

Katherine Woods
Associate Editor, EJETS
Director, Eridanus Planetary Museum of Natural History
Eridanus

(Editor's note: transmission dated May 17, 2152; Message published January 09, 2163. This publication, after much discussion by the editorial board, was approved for the benefit of the scientific community. This note does not constitute a validation of the lingua system, nor of the publication of new names or combinations previously correctly published outside the IJSE.)

CELESTIAL POLICE

LOGAN BRENNER

"*T*hank you for joining the second formulation of the Celestial Police."

Jessica Dalton, the Administrator of the National Aeronautics and Space Administration, began her speech halfheartedly looking into a sea of faces dotted with eyes glazed over. The group of scientists from leading research institutions and universities knew why they were there, so only about fifty percent of the people were happy to provide Jessica with the formality of their physical presence in the room.

The other half of the attendees were trying to choose one of the many bullet points whirring by on their mental list of excuses to leave. She knew that some must have settled on the name of committee as reason enough to not take their charge seriously. They did everything they could to silently communicate that they wanted to be anywhere but there using glares, crossed arms, and pursed lips. She was also trying to figure out which half of the room she would have belonged in if she were on the other side of the podium. Regardless, everyone there had agreed to be a part of the Celestial Police.

"Celestial Police, Himmelspolizei in German, first convened 300 years ago in 1800. The 24 members invited by

Baron Franz Xaver von Zach gathered near Bremen, Germany with the purpose of finding the missing planet between Mars and Jupiter. As you all well know, there is no planet between Mars and Jupiter; instead we have the asteroid belt, a failed planet, with which we are going to become better acquainted with soon."

The corny disaster movies of the past are becoming our present, Jessica thought. The asteroid belt is falling out of orbit and Ceres, Vesta, Pallas, and Hygiea are rocketing toward Earth.

In retrospect, Jessica realized she could have named the committee differently. It seemed funny when they thought they could redirect the major asteroids, which was only a few weeks ago, but with a strike imminent it was cruel to name the committee in honor of the group of men who first searched for what would soon mean certain doom. On the meeting invitation she tried to craft some verbiage that made the title Celestial Police seem more empowering than anything else, that this group of people was going to do whatever they could to make Earth's remaining existence pleasant. Maybe she should have named them the Morphine Drip Club. Something light but with a little less irony.

In the split second it took for her to take a breath Jessica recalled her conversation with the President a few months prior and again felt the full weight of what he said. He was governing a tired nation, a group of people living with the burden of knowing too much. The President's best response to the national melancholia was to stop reporting the bad news. People were already told what was coming, so further communications should be accompanied by a sugary, cavity-inducing candy coating to make swallowing updates on their dismal situation a little easier. He described his plan to Jessica by comparing it to a series of exponentially depressing examples. When you put down a pet you know the end is near, but you still have that last day where you give it everything it wants. Or giving a death row prisoner a last meal. Or travelling around the world with a loved one that has a terminal illness. You check off that bucket list as best you can. He said we should go out with a bang, then quickly looked down embarrassed by his unintentional pun.

"Executive order 20,568 was issued 3 months ago. President Reynolds is asking us to fundamentally alter how we report our scientific research because he is genuinely concerned about the collective state of mind of the planet. So let me get to it. Federally funded research must suppress publication of data that can be interpreted in a negative light. That is not to say that it cannot be published at all, but everything will be in password protected federal journals, what we are calling the electronic vault."

Unlike their historical counterparts, the members of the Celestial Police weren't policing the sky looking for celestial objects; they were policing the literature. Under typical conditions, proponents of free speech would have fought against this, but everyone was in uncharted waters and were willing to forgo some basic freedoms if it meant producing a bit more serotonin. The government was clearly hijacking scientists' research but looking out into the crowd most people looked relieved. Scientists were tired of the backlash they regularly incurred by publishing their objective research findings. Their work on the asteroid strikes was constantly assaulted by the half brained journalists and politicians who disliked being the bearers of bad news. To avoid a shoot the messenger scenario, journalists and politicians were denigrating the research to make the situation seem less certain than it actually is, introducing unfounded doubt fueled by fear.

Jessica had been wondering if the modern mental health professionals had codified the steps of grief due to asteroid strike to update the Kübler-Ross model. They had been through the shock, followed by the protesting phase, which was sometimes denial and sometimes bargaining, although she wasn't sure what peaceful assembly would do to sway the trajectory of an asteroid. Then came the anger manifesting itself as looting, which transitioned into the euphoria phase during which everyone fulfilled their greatest desires and doesn't have an exact corollary in the traditional grieving steps. People had now settled into depression so the goal of the executive order was to try and get everyone to acceptance and enjoy what time was left. But maybe everyone was depressed because they had already reached acceptance.

So, she committed to the President's mission of softening science with a little whimsy to give the public some carefree days. She wondered if the scientific community had a responsibility to keep reporting. Models and tests failed to yield positive results so maybe sharing this news wasn't actually helping anyone. She questioned whether knowledge truly was power in this situation. However, is it up to the President and the few people in this room to decide what is best for everyone? She wished there was a way to poll the world to find out who wanted more information and only communicate the updates, however bleak, with them. Leave the people who wanted to exist in their little bubble alone. She didn't blame the bubble people and half-wondered what box she would check in the hypothetical poll. She was unprepared for this self-reflection and the pause in her speech was longer than intended.

"This will be a short meeting, I don't want to keep you any longer than necessary. When you leave you will be given a packet of information on how to report your science to different outlets. There are electronic templates for various methods of communication, journals, books, newspaper articles, even social media. This will all be very easy, you won't even need to think about it. If you are interested in contributing un-redacted results to the electronic vault there is a template for that as well. If there are no questions you are all free to go."

Of course there were no questions. There was a combination of anger, sadness, and relief on the faces that were now filing out the door. Everyone in the room was tired of being an angel of death and now they had a get out of jail free card. They could keep their mouths shut. Still struggling with whether it was her duty to report the painful truth, Jessica didn't know if she would be able to cash in her card.

Considering the circumstances Jessica thought the meeting went well. Although she still wasn't sure if it was the morally correct thing to do, she did feel some relief knowing that she wouldn't have to send out a press release of her model's current run. She returned to her computer to examine the latest projection for impact. Her computer code was riddled with silly names for each command. Making her code sound like a video game helped her dissociate a bit from the reality of the situation. Some people found this a useful coping mechanism. Others refused to execute it because they were offended by what they considered a lack of seriousness from the Administrator of NASA. Lucky for Jessica, interpersonal office drama was pretty low on her list of things that could ruin her day.

Back at her desk, her code had been spitting out startling numbers. Today they were within error of impact. Before she could pull up the electronic template for the data vault there was a deafening bang and a bright light filled her eyes.

Jessica jolted and quickly picked her head up from the desk. Her neck was stiff and she was disoriented by the fan of papers in front of her. A security guard was banging on her office door holding a flashlight to the glass. It was midnight and it was time to lock up the campus. Jessica peeled off the latest comments from reviewer three that were stuck to her cheek and stood up to go home. Reviews were due in two days.

CHANKRA'S HANDS

CRYSTAL RILEY

Author's note:
This story may seem hard to read, rambling, or lacking a plot. Please be forgiving, a robot generated this story (with a little grammatical help from a human).

Input parameters:

NUM CHARACTERS: 3
CHARACTERS: Zmorg'tl, Chankra, Dr. Mak'reng
FREQUENCY DEPTH: 4
STORY LENGTH LIMIT: 1500
NON EXISTENT SEED: the

If you're curious how it works:

This begins with a webcrawler. This webcrawler walked through the Document Object Model (DOM) of the first 3 links on Google for the query "science fiction story" with depth 5, meaning if the webcrawler found a link, it would only follow 5 links from the original page, looking for stories. A story was defined as any group of text in the same DOM element that had a word count of greater than 1000 words. This collection of stories were scraped and organized as a json. The webcrawler discovered 753 unique stories.

A dictionary of words was used to locate proper nouns, by assuming any word beginning with a capital letter that was not in the dictionary was assumed to be a character name, a place, or an unusual thing. All proper nouns were replaced by a special character.

A frequency map was then created of all the words in the scraped stories. This frequency map mapped every word to all the words that follow that word and the frequency of which that the following word followed. This frequency map was then used to generate an original story. A seed was chosen to start the story by randomly choosing a word in the frequency map. The list of "following words" was then randomly chosen, weighted by the frequency that it followed the previous word. This frequency map of parametrized depth was used to determine the probability distribution for the next word. If a word path was ever chosen that had no words to follow it (such as the last word in a story or an incredibly rare combination of depth words), the seed word "the" was then used. This continued until the story length limit was reached.

This generated a story that still had the special character in place of all the characters and places. A random letter generator weighed by the frequency of use in the English language generated character names. The story was read by a human reader to remove all partial sentences. Creative liberty was then taken to assign the specially marked proper nouns to the character names. Lastly, a final human read was done to fix any spelling or grammar.

Voila.

CHANKRA'S HANDS

❖ ❖ ❖

"**T**have to supply swings?" questioned Zmorg'tl, the realer of the two from that whirled alcove. He comes sometimes but we are turning to follow, in time, to teach trading to Chankra. Dr. Mak'reng squealed, "I'm sure it's entirely in." Chankra swore indiscernibly on her spare hand she forged from a pile of hesitant bolts.

It interrupted her, "Where face supersonic own minutes?" She shot a mean look at Zmorg'tl. Her hand continued, "Stream. Understand." Dr. Mak'reng had her characteristic college vehemence. Dr. Mak'reng wanted to study Chankra. Her desire was not new. Chankra was bending, in a dark way.

Zmorg'tl spotted the interest in Dr. Mak'reng eyes as she concentrated on Chankra, "Take the swing with you," Zmorg'tl annoyingly breathed.

"Was Chankra's from before she was cracked away," retorted Dr. Mak'reng.

"It's just, her hands," she continued. Zmorg'tl holding his own heads walked off, rolling all of his eyes. This mission would never be completed. Tons and tons were gone. The rest seemed to have access down. They were alone, but they did not yet know. Zmorg'tl had arms skinny. It quite often happens. There were strands of magnetic tape wherever he had been.

Zmorg'tl was from an alcove, where most had a free head. He had taken up rocketry with his spare heads and nights. He remembered about there. He forget the name. His heart dead, his idea is worth so much and if he woke his head to participate? All his excess brainpower wasted. The first heavy lab he had saw hands. The image lifted him. He was jealous because he only had many heads, but no hands. His jealousy feed the rawness of his allowed bloom. Now he is wasteful of his head and his feet.

Dr. Mak'reng had prepared to sit. She didn't often. "You must sit with me. We have massive nice chairs of bursting out body wires," she stated toward Chankra. Her invite wasn't working. She and Chankra still stared at robot hand. Dr. Mak'reng started a monologue, her arrogance dripping, Chankra didn't listen:

"… as us, especially me, as I huddle into myself, the young age of fifteen, a genius. From the top of the class, there has always been I. My life couldn't air a coming, but I can do a lot of feel. Unlike you robots. Oh, to be younger, the turned list of things I wanted. Gait, waiting fame, home, breasts, a 'Yes,' to an offer, or smiling. When I cared only about grades and betraying a gentleman's wedding. And grooming. Welcome people wrapped in stale iron, is this a complete story to tell of peace?"

Dr. Mak'reng stopped abruptly. She remembered her purpose… the peace.

Chankra looked like she were about to let a wail. The specialists of her existence said the day she was created, "With high assurance, the moment she matures, she'll speak again." Dr. Mak'reng heard of this in her studies and took charge to perfume and boat to find her. Dr. Mak'reng, for years, considered if she had DNA. The history's and say-ings? Dr. Mak'reng knew down deep that Chankra would be the first.

Zmorg'tl tapped the glass. "Are we really completely alone?" he said towards the window, paranoia in his voice.

"I'm busy, can't you see, idiot?" answered Dr. Mak'reng. "Chankra is of different world... it's been said that she knows every moment from the very beginning of thought. From all alien ways."

"I'm an alien to you, human," trailed Zmorg'tl.

"Not an interesting one," insulted Dr. Mak'reng.

She approached Chankra. "C'mon your pattern projec-tion is to stay symmetrical..." she consoled as she soothed. Chankra was so burnt she really had looks of ground-to-powder marking her in a single, large gape. Adolescence did not treat her well. She hadn't developed a full range of words. Thinking, however, she did well. Her few words she had were chanting through her mind. She though of sty-rofoam for sure. The oil and blood that had fell down it in the floods. Zmort'tl tapped his finger and licked it, "lime-flavored."

Dr. Mak'reng had gotten so close, she was virtually shin-ing; there she was ugly. "More cotton than glass hands," she exclaimed when Chankra closed the distance. Dr. Mak'reng had never met such a creature, her upper and lower robot. She was staring at Chankra's right one, a time-released valve with great, monumental grip. Dr. Mak'reng screams echoed through their shack. Zmorg'tl lazily went over. "You made her upset. She moved like that because I looked at her hovercraft." This soil landing would not be the end of Dr. Mak'reng. Chankra released. Dr. Mak'reng climbed jittering away.

Various components of Chankra murmured. Zmorg'tl glared at Dr. Mak'reng as he hoped she'd know what to do next. "That flare must have started itself. She has more power than the sun itself," the doctor's voice shaked.

THE LAST APE OF HERZOG'S JEWEL

NATHAN FREDRICKSON

*T*omorrow morning the reconstructors will come and rip apart every molecule on the planet. On *my* planet. I built the autoplants. I built the geothermal stations. I built the highways to the new settlements, and I remember when they were just tents and prefabs. I am the last living vat-grown, robot-raised, Child-of-Earth on Herzog's Jewel and that used to mean something, damn it. Hell, they even named the planet after me. And now. Look at my people dancing in the streets, the ingrates. On the night of my government's bicentennial, no less. This was supposed to be my celebration. A celebration of stability, of order, of peace, of life. And now the whole planet is whooping and hollering and pissing all over it. I can only assume that our vile "cousins" had planned to hold the referendum today. They aren't lying about their intelligence; always ten steps ahead...

The referendum was today. It's hard to believe. The day's felt like a decade. And those grey slabs from Earth - or what's left of it—might as well have been hanging in my skies for a lifetime. And I've lived a damn long time, as anyone on this as-of-yet still material world will tell you. Not that age means anything to *them*. The one who spelled it all out for me claimed to have had a "continuity of conscious-ness" for one thousand, three hundred and fifty two years. Notice how they don't use the words "living" or "alive." God, I'll never forget the smirk on that thing's virtual face when it told me that we were literally cousins. It even had this ge-nealogy it had conjured up on a massive vellum scroll - its idea of a joke, I imagine. But as far as I'm concerned, all of my cousins from Earth died when they decided to demol-ish themselves into thinking dust. And today my people decided to do the same. I've always suspected that democ-racy was a bad idea.

How could they trust those flying bricks? How could they trust something that needs to install a brain implant just so they can talk to you face to face? I don't even think they're really from Earth. There's no way they could have made it from Sol on the timeline they're talking about - not without breaking the light barrier, and my top physicists as-sure me that such a thing is impossible. Assured. I imagine they're all drunk and lighting things on fire like the rest of the rabble now. They're all fools. Yes, our cold visitors knew everything we knew about Earth and more. Yes, they could speak mother-languages that our linguists had tried to re-construct, and all other kinds of strange bastard creoles that made a sort of sense. I admit that even their virtual plazas could be quite pleasing to the human eye, assuming you were able to forget where you really were; or *weren't* if we're being precise. But seeing isn't believing when your sight is nothing more than nanites tickling your optic nerve. If our so-called cousins are as smart as they seem to be, then who's to say this isn't some elaborate hoax? My bet is that these "reunion drones" blocking my white sunlight are little more than alien von Neumann probes, staking out an easy mining operation for their evil empire. I bet some tentacled monster is sitting in a palace lightyears away, burping to itself in amusement, "We told them we were bringing utopia, the stupid apes."

Utopia. What a joke. The only good thing to come out of this mess is the delightful little irony we've gleaned from our vile cousins' gift of a complete Greek lexicon. No Place indeed. This planet is the only paradise I care about. I said as much in their virtual debates. I want the pleasure of waking at dawn to calibrate my farming drones, I said. I want to smell the dirt of Herzog's Jewel on every carrot, beet and onion, I said. I want to savor the fruits of a day's work, damn it, not wave my hand and have my absent whims appear on a machine's idea of a dinner table. Of course it was the bastard with the ridiculous scroll they put on the other podium. I've been replaying the record all night.

"In the world we're offering, you could do all of that, simulated down to the last atom. You could put temporary limits on your memory; you wouldn't know you had been translated into code. You could even harvest the crops yourself, if you're so suspicious of technology." The whole damn planet loved that. Every man, woman and child. I can imagine their bodies slack-jawed and drooling in the houses I made possible while their intoxicated minds simulated laughter in their world. The new world. It will be the new world. There's no stopping it now.

Every vote, "yes." Every single soul on the Jewel except for old Governor Herzog. That's what really gets me. I could almost accept defeat with a loyal troop who still loves their bodies. Just ten percent of the planet, even. But no. I am the only one who won't be scanned, ripped and downloaded willingly.

I blame the youth. There's something perverse about sexual reproduction that encourages decadence. I've always said so, but Earth's fate proves it beyond any doubt. In my prime all ten thousand of us were perfectly curated zygotes grown in incubators like our parents intended. We never worried about anything as backwards as sexual selection. The last technology from Earth that I ever trusted was their three generation reproduction plan. Now that was a feat of human ingenuity. A population over a million strong by the fourth generation. Optimal genetic diversity. Negligible risks of genetic disease or complications from inbreeding. An average increase of ten IQ points per person. I can't believe that it was my signature that legalized sex. That was always the plan, of course, but I could have stopped it. Now these damn kids are getting their disgusting fluids all over my streets and spitting the word eugenics like it's some kind of curse. Eugenics. They wouldn't even know the word if it wasn't for the so-called Earthlings, those hypocrites. Who do those womb-born think planned my generation, the nursery robots? All it took was one manipulative simulation of the Earth calendar's 20th century, and suddenly every child under the age of fifty thinks I'm some kind of goose-stepping monster. If I had continued the reproduction plans for another three generations, the population would have been nice and orderly. Smarter, anyway. Too smart for any of this nonsense. More like the old days. The simpler days.

Yes, there was pain. The youth forget that a planet as lush as this one will inevitably evolve its share of megafauna and pack carnivores. Maybe it's our fault for driving the worst of them to extinction. Looking at the fires in the city below, I long for the days of the jungle. At least then you knew the danger. You could face your opponent head on, mass accelerator in hand. When you saw the glowing eyes in the brush, you could see the soul of the beast, knew that the only thing that drove it was hunger. But you can't look into the eyes of these bodiless invaders. When we tamed the frontiers we discovered who we really were, what it meant to be human. But all we left for our descendants was unearned luxury and ennui. No wonder they're so obsessed with utopia.

Maybe when the solar system is computronium I'll relive those days. Maybe I'll get it right this time. The goal never should have been Earth's comforts, it should have been glorious struggle on my eternally green jewel. Maybe I'll make an infinite jungle, so for every canopy we pave over, there will be another wilderness in every direction. Or maybe I'll spin up a new Earth, show the bastards what a real homeworld should look like. There are a lot of intriguing possibilities in the archives our cousins brought. Apparently Stone Age societies lived in jungles like ours well into Earth's industrial period. I suspect that this "historical data" is just another joke, a prod at my perceived backwardness. But in the new world, history is what we make it, right? Isn't that what the things from Earth said? Real or not I want to be one of the jungle people. I'll rip off all of my jackets and medals and tassels and raiments. I'll harden wood spears in my precious fire and hunt for my own pelts. The sex will be distasteful... but I suppose I could ensure the placement of incubation centers on my new Earth. Yes, I could start a new reproduction plan. In three more generations a horde of beautiful geniuses will spill out of the Amazon, smashing every machine more complicated than a pulley with their perfect stone axes.

I suppose that will mean no more mansion, though. I admit that for all of my nostalgia I can't help but love the towers, the terraced gardens, the kitchens. But I have worked for those comforts. I've served the prosperity of the planet for two hundred years, I deserve personal prosperity. I guess my jungle empire to come could always build new governor's mansions. But I've already put in my time. How will I resist the temptation to shout a command and find these old halls plucked out from the air in front of me? I don't want another god-damned two hundred years of public service to reach the conditions necessary to build this sort of public project. But I can't just summon the thing. That's cheating, isn't it? Can I sleep soundly in an atom-for-atom replica of my bed? What dreams will come when I become the dream of a solar brain?

I've never been so anxious. Maybe the pump where my heart was will fail and I'll keel over before the reconstructors get here. What a laugh that would be. The one thing those bricks couldn't control: the body of their last enemy clutching his chest and smiling as the nanites eat his corpse. My cousin claimed that people of the new world could bring anyone back to life with sufficient data. He said that all they would need was a journal, old stories, a scrap of clothing and a lock of hair - something like that. A fresh corpse would probably be more than enough to drag me from their idea of hell into mine. But that euphemism for life he always used - "continuity of consciousness" - would I have that? All I can picture is an army of the living dead; philosophical zombies that offer a convincing illusion. That's the problem, isn't it: convincing illusions. When they rip me apart maybe it will just be an automaton that takes my place. The new Governor Herzog will be a thief made out of code, living with my stolen memories. They say that when we are uploaded, we will simultaneously experience being embodied and disembodied until our brain is completely digitized in order to ensure a "smooth transition." But that won't happen if I die first. And even if I live through the conversion, the question of "me" will be boundless. I talked to one of the Earthlings who had lived before the first reconstruction. She said that she'd lived the last century as a starfish, and then a god-damned tesseract appeared out of nowhere and called her a stodgy old reactionary.

I'm probably just an ape in their eyes. Worse than a primitive. An animal. They talked to all of us like we were pets, really. Always with their condescending smiles and pats on the shoulder, their promises to guide us in "what must be a frightening time." The starfish woman has the most integrity of all of them. I should follow her lead. They think I'm an animal now. They haven't seen what horrors wait in this skull. I'll give myself a thousand arms and a coat of spines, six tons of muscle and bones made out of stone. I'll crash into whatever they call a home and rip and tear until they have to break their promise that they will never end a life. Maybe I could trick them that way. I'll be so destructive that they'll either have to allow the sin of death, or print me a new body in the old world, throw me on a planet somewhere to fend for myself. Then I'll stack all of the primordial muck into clay soldiers and crown myself the emperor of mud.

Dawn should come any minute now. The hollering below has stopped, for the most part. The street lights that aren't broken are catching less smoke in their beams. The Earthlings set up "translation centers" for anyone who wanted to be reconstructed before the zero-hour. I can see a line of my people now. Lord, there are thousands of them. It reminds me of the last days of the super-predators. Once proud animals, now docile, now marching to a room where their bodies will be destroyed. At least the predators got the peace of death: the only thing they themselves had ever offered to the universe. But none of the apes below can really guess what awaits them in those Earth slaughterhouses. We were builders, and now our cousins will build us. Even if it is really *us* emerging in the new world, we won't build when everything is possible. We will become lines of flight through infinite worlds infinitely re-made. We will drift in a virtual foam, and actualize only what we see. We will either be bubbles of our self-indulgent imagination, or be erased in a sea of consciousness that none of us can possibly understand. All I can do now is pour a stiff drink and watch the last sunrise on my jewel. I think I'll do that for the next century.

THE MEN AND THE STARS: A SPEECH FROM THE FUTURE

IVAN GLAUCIO PAULINO-LIMA

*T*oday, we celebrate greatness. The achievements of human kind have accumulated through millennia, have generated the science and the technology that brought us here. We are now sending a message from Mars to the people of our home world. Today will be remembered as the tipping point for the expansion of human kind into the vastness of space. We have left our cosmic island to scout new worlds. This is not only about the future, the past, or the present. It concerns the whole history of humanity, the entire history of life as we know it.

Today is a special day. This moment is larger than just stepping on the surface of Mars. The legendary astronaut Betsie Phoenix would give everything to be here today. And she is. She used to tell the story of a little girl she met a long time ago. I remember as if it was today when she asked me:

"You see that star there?"

"The one that is moving?"

"Exactly, that is actually not a star."

"How do you know?"

"Because I've been there."

"What? How is that even possible?"

"It is a satellite."

"You've been inside a satellite?"

"Yes, in a big one. This satellite is a space station. It is called the International Space Station. Built through the efforts of many nations."

I was only six years old when I came to realize that not all of the pin pricks of light we see in the night sky are truly stars. Some are planets, some are meteors, and still others are *man-made* satellites.

This memory makes me think that in a sense, men have already reached the stars. We made our own stars. Human spirit propelled us to set foot on Selene and Ares—or Luna and Mars, as you wish. How is that for an encounter with the divine? We are still dealing with this expansion of the mind.

In a few moments another world will gain human footprints. This single event will start another geological era here, one that we are all a part of. It is not only an individual who will be soon walking on Mars. It is an entire species from a foreign place, from a foreign time. We have new responsibilities now. A cosmic perspective is not a luxury anymore. It is absolutely necessary to secure our place in the cosmos.

The critical Entry-Descent-Landing process has just passed and yes, it was scary. But our fear does not compare with our excitement of actually building this moment.

It is almost time to go. We must open this door before

sunrise. We don't want to miss the spectacle for the dawn of men. Outside this door a world of possibilities awaits. Let us prepare. *Ad astra* and godspeed.

A LITTLE OCEAN BREEZE

SANJOY M. SOM

May 10th, 2027

"Stuck? What do you mean, 'stuck?'" snapped Douglas Manchester, in his unmistakable North Yorkshire accent.

A deep, composed voice answered. "Doug, all thrusters are engaged, and we're not going anywhere." Chief pilot James N'kuso kept his focus out of the front porthole, his thumbs on the joysticks that controlled the throttle and orientation of the submersible's thrusters.

A mile and half under the Pacific Ocean in the Deep Submergence Vehicle *Pytheas*, engineer Doug Manchester, pilot James N'kuso, and dive scientist Ryan Romano were investigating the increased earthquake activity at the undersea Axial Volcano on the Juan the Fuca ridge, an oceanic mountainous spine on the seafloor about two hundred miles west of Seattle, Washington. Their mission was to collect the superheated water gushing out of black smoker vents located in the volcanic crater walls. They had just gently landed on a flat ridge nearby a smoker called *El Guapo*, when *Pytheas* jerked and sat tilted.

"I think we have bigger problems…" mumbled Romano,

eerily calm, concentrating her gaze on the screen that relayed what the *Pytheas* starboard camera was capturing. "Look, we cracked the ocean crust and… Oh, *merda…*"

Both Manchester and N'kuso stared at the screen, in silence, for a few seconds, as yellow ooze emerged from the cracked, black, lava-rock veneer, and wrapped itself around the submersible's struts.

"Molten sulfur. We hit molten sulfur, which is solidifying as it's exposed to the cold seawater. We're going to be glued here," she calmly uttered, careful to not reveal her fright.

As N'kuso reached for the hydrophone; electronic static signaled its liveness, "*Pytheas* abort. Abort. Axial is erupting."

"Drop the weights."

Four days earlier

"Woah," awed Manchester, as their autonomous vehicle entered the span of the Astoria Bridge. The bridge crossed the mighty Columbia River separating the states of Oregon and Washington in the United States. Built as a steel cantilever-through-truss bridge spanning four miles and reaching over two hundred feet above the river, the green-painted Astoria-Megler bridge was as aesthetically beautiful as it was imposing.

"My favorite part of the drive," proclaimed veteran astronaut Sonali Williams, breaking the awestricken silence. "We'll be in Astoria in ten minutes."

"Almost as pretty as Tower Bridge on the Thames," beamed Manchester. Williams shook her head, yet she betrayed a smile. The eager Englishman amused her. Despite their dizzying height as they crossed the cantilever, both noted the choppy waters and dark clouds looming on the horizon of the Pacific ocean.

"It's going to be a bumpy ride," frowned Williams gesturing toward the impending storm in the distance. Manchester was sitting opposite her twiddling the ring on his finger, revealing his excitement. The autonomous vehicle exited the highway onto the off-ramp that guided them into the sleepy town of Astoria, Oregon.

"A little ocean breeze won't keep a chopper down," said Doug with optimism.

It was a gusty afternoon in the town Scarborough in North Yorkshire, England, when eight-year-old Doug Manchester fell off the boardwalk into the frigid bay fifteen feet below. A careless step. He was playing with the balsa wood and paper airplane he had built that morning with his grandfather, a local butcher. The plane caught the perfect air current and floated away from his hand. His creation, in its wave-like glide, slowly increased speed and altitude. He ran after it knowing the road ended at the boardwalk, but he had failed to notice that a construction crew had moved some of the cobble-stones that made up the road to reach a few rotten wooden piers below. His eyes followed the plane, and his feet caught a precarious stone as he reached the boardwalk. In a futile attempt to regain his balance, he stumbled forward, his arms flailing chaotically, and with a scream, he fumbled into the waters below—

Peeking through his exhausted eyes, he noticed the room still spinning. His clothes were neatly folded on a chair next to his bed. His vision slowly cleared, and the silhouette of a man crystallized to reveal his grandfather staring down. Doug's head throbbed.

"You're a lucky little chopper, Douggie. Me mate, James, fished you out of the soup. You were out like a crab on ice. This isn't Liverpool." He dabbed a wet rag on Doug's forehead. It stung. "You need to be more careful, boy," he said pedantically. The elderly man then smiled wide and pinched Doug's cheek and shook it, "but no little ocean breeze will keep my chopper down, eh?" He patted his grandson affectionately.

Williams threw her duffel bag on the hotel room bed, and sauntered to the faded window overlooking the sailboat-filled Astoria marina. Rain started pattering against the glass. She was gazing just beyond the wooden docks when two short vibrations from her wrist watch distracted her trance. "Beers?" the message read. She audibly smirked, pressed the small screen, waited for the short pulse, and then replied vocally, "We're meeting Jim at 7pm, so let's meet in the lobby fifteen minutes before." As she removed her finger, her words transcribed and flew into the ether to appear a moment later on Manchester's watch. Disappointment etched his face. She turned away from the overlook leaving the raindrops to pelt the window in her absence, tossed her watch on the bed, and started the faucet for a bath. She had been awaiting this moment of relaxation since leaving NASA's Johnson Space Center for Portland eight hours earlier.

Douglas Manchester, from the European Space Agency, and Sonali Williams from NASA, were in Astoria because both were expected the next day onboard *Sea Orbiter II*, an engineering masterpiece dedicated to exploring the world's oceans. As a newly selected astronaut, Manchester was sent by ESA as part of his 'operations in confined environments' training. Williams, a veteran of two spaceflights, was sent to study the operational logistics of the vessel as part of an internal NASA study for deep-space exploration. They would be flown by helicopter to the vessel, which was located at the site of the Axial undersea volcano, twenty-four hours by ship due west from the Oregon Coast. Manchester and Williams had only just met earlier this day after they both landed in Portland. Following a few pleasant email exchanges after first hearing of their assignment, they had been looking forward to getting to know each other. An engaging conversation ensued during the two hour drive from Portland to Astoria as they enthusiastically acquainted themselves.

The Old Salt tavern was an unremarkable brick structure from the outside. The sole, run-down building near the docks had been a local favorite for decades. The pouring rain was streaking diagonally in the light of the few dim lanterns swaying back and forth from the roof spillway. Night had fallen suddenly due to the storm clouds shading the sky. Muffled music emanated from the building. A narrow, green door next to a partially washed out, black chalkboard which had earlier in the day listed happy-hour specials, revealed the entrance. *This place seems stuck in time*, thought Williams. She shoved the heavy door open. The sudden blast of music filled her ears, and unexpectedly thick, warm air invaded her lungs. She led Manchester as they made their way through the maze of people toward the bar.

"Just like home." He breathed through a comfortable smile.

"That must be Jim," pointed Williams through the crowd as they entered the tavern. Her eyes were stinging from the acrid air.

"Aye," Manchester nodded. James 'Jim' N'kuso was the sole African American sitting at the bar.

As Williams and Manchester approached, the man turned towards them and nodded upwards without a change in facial expression, whispering to himself, "And here come the space cadets…"

"Jim N'kuso?" she awaited his positive reply before continuing, "Sonali Williams, NASA, and this is—"

"Doug Manchester," exclaimed the Englishman jovially thrusting his hand forward, "How do you do?"

N'kuso stood as he took Manchester's hand with a facial expression revealing his mild amusement. Williams shrugged.

"Drs. Williams, Manchester, it's nice to meet you both. Let's take that table there before someone snatches it." Despite hints of U.S. east coast, neither Manchester nor Williams could figure out where his accent stemmed from. He pointed with a pint in hand as he led them to a standing table by the jukebox. Manchester noted the dark color of the brew. He caught a whiff of hops. *Good taste*, he said to himself.

N'kuso briefed them on the helicopter pickup scheduled for the next day. *Sea Orbiter II* housed a winged chopper for scientific reconnaissance missions, and shuttled personnel to and from the deep-sea vessel. The vessel could only dock at deep water ports due to its remarkable size. He then continued to Manchester's role on the mission: to dive into the caldera of the submarine Axial Volcano on *Sea Orbiter II*'s human-rated deep-submergence vehicle, *Pytheas*.

"This is not going to be a typical seafloor exploration mission," said N'kuso. "Seismometers on the ocean floor indicate high levels of earthquake activity, and the seafloor water-pressure sensors are consistent with inflation." He spoke loudly to overcome *Deep Purple's* screeching guitar as 'Smoke on the Water' blared through the bar's speakers.

"Inflation of what?" replied Manchester, loudly. His arms were folded on the table as he leaned forwards to capture as much of N'kuso's answer as possible.

"My bad." N'kuso quickly added, "I'm used to speaking with scientists. Y'all are both engineers, yes? Anyway, inflation means that magma pressure from the volcano is pushing the seafloor upwards," he clarified while his interlaced fingers gestured a rising dome. "This shortens the water column—the amount of water— above the volcano," he described with his palms facing each horizontally. "This decreases the pressure that is recorded by the instruments on the seafloor."

Williams sat nodding. "What does this mean?" interrupted Manchester.

"Not sure to be honest," responded N'kuso in the short lull in between songs. "A similar but stronger sequence of events happened three months ago, but dissipated. This one might too; we just don't know. But the hydrothermal vent scientists are damn excited."

Sonali Williams first learned about hydrothermal vents as a chemistry student at St. Xavier's College in Kolkata, India. Her undergraduate thesis examined such vents. After obtaining a fellowship to study abroad from the Indian government, she continued her education at the Monterey Bay Aquarium Research Institute in Monterey, California, working on autonomous ocean-mapping robots. In her Kolkata classroom, she had learned that Axial Seamount is a one-thousand-foot high volcano located 4,600 feet below the surface of the ocean. It sits on the Juan the Fuca ridge, an underwater mountainous spine marking the boundary between the massive Pacific plate and the last sliver of another tectonic plate that is disappearing below North

America through the geological process of subduction. Her eyes widened when she realized that this same mechanism is responsible for creating the volcanoes that pepper the US Pacific Northwest, such as Mount Rainier and Mount Saint Helens, which famously erupted in 1980. Williams read that this small plate is pulling away, like stretched taffy, from the Pacific plate as it sinks, creating a region of thin ocean crust.

She spent countless hours in the suffocating reading room of the library as wobbly fans swirled overhead. She read about how this thin crust allows magma and ocean water to coexist in close proximity, giving rise to *black smokers*—towering chimneys of rock known as hydrothermal vents. With thrill, she learned that historically, lava had oozed out on the seafloor during underwater eruptions inside, and near, Axial Seamount's summit crater. The chemical processes that befalls ocean water as it interacts with ocean crust was what interested her most. She learned that the water's temperature increased from the frigid 2°C of the ocean floor to several hundred degrees as it interacts with the hot rocks a few miles above a molten pool of magma brought near the surface by the pulling of the tectonic plates.

As she flipped the pages of the frumpy textbook, she soaked in readily how the hot water absorbs magma-released sulfur and dissolves elements like iron from minerals during its journey through rock. She had to read several times the section that described how the resulting super-heated jet of water that emerges violently from the sea-floor into the cold ocean produces a black smoke—dark metal-sulfide particles, really—and new unpronounceable minerals that crystallize to form the chimney's walls. These cathedral spires tower tens of feet above the ocean floor.

The helicopter punched through the clouds, and *Sea Orbiter II* revealed itself as a scintillating white disk proudly emerging from the vast ocean blue. The majestic swan-like vessel seemed unbothered by the rough waves that pounded her hull. Both Williams and Manchester, weary from their four hour helicopter ride, opened their eyes wide and forgot their tiredness. N'kuso smiled at their reactions. "Ain't she something?" he quipped proudly.

"Pictures don't do justice," responded Manchester.

Williams estimated the vessel to be at least twelve stories high. The saucer shaped base was above sea-level to expose the helipad, but she couldn't perceive how far into the water the vessel extended.

Manchester could almost feel the swan welcoming them as the pilot did a full circle of the ship before flying by the 'eye' of the vessel—the bridge. She maneuvered the chopper into a descent toward the landing platform located at the base of the 'neck'. They were close enough that Williams could discern individual people behind the windows as they flew by. The pilot skillfully placed the helicopter down on the pad despite the obviously powerful wind gusts. *A little ocean breeze won't keep a chopper down,* Manchester mused, as the helicopter struts gently connected with the helipad. The giant aluminum-magnesium beast hardly noticed the little hummingbird landing between its broad shoulder blades.

"Welcome aboard," Williams and Manchester turned as they both stepped out of the helicopter whose whizzing blades sprayed water mist around them. A few of these droplets stung Williams' face. Manchester didn't seem to notice, as he was protected from the elements by his russet beard. A tall, thin, dark-haired woman was confidently walking towards them. Her short hair didn't seem affected by the wind, as if transfixed by the water spray. A few wrinkles jetted away from behind her thick-rimmed rectangular glasses. Her hand was rising to offer a shake, her accent unmistakably Italian.

Williams met the stranger's eyes and hand and firmly replied with an assertive, "Thank you."

"My name is Ryan Romano," she invited as they walked towards the bay at the base of the towering neck that was to house the helicopter. Manchester reveled in her rolling R's. "I will be your scientific escort while you are here." After they had entered the vessel, Romano shut the watertight hatch behind them. Manchester only now noticed her powerful green eyes that contained flares of orange. "I see you have met James. He always volunteers to pick up people in Astoria. He keeps boasting about that old pub. What is it called? A terrible place, really, suitable only for claustrophobia-tolerant submarine pilots."

"Ain't the *Piazza Navona*, for sure," jested N'kuso laughing, referring to the large cobblestone plaza in Rome boasting the Fountain of the Four Rivers, and, as Romano had described, the best place in the world to enjoy a sweet martini on a warm summer's day.

"You didn't tell us you were a sub pilot," piped Manchester excitedly.

"I also collect stamps, what else do you want to know?" smirked N'kuso.

Manchester lifted his finger and started to form a retort when N'kuso cut him off, "Just kidding. See you two tomorrow." He nodded to Romano and took leave of the group.

Romano added, "He will be our pilot when we go down. A good thing too—best one on board," she beamed. Manchester was pondering how one would earn a reputation for being a 'bad submarine pilot', but Romano interrupted his day dreaming. "Let me show you to your quarters. We'll be in the lower deck quarters near the labs."

"Blimey," exclaimed Manchester as they entered their suite. "I was not expecting a window." They entered to a semicircular arrangement of white couches facing away from the door they had just opened, towards a large elliptical window as wide as the room. An agitated ocean churned behind it; particulates suspended in the water could be seen dancing beyond the glass.

"You are lucky," said Romano matter-of-factly. "In the current ship's configuration, we are about five meters below sea level hence the beautiful blue you are seeing, but given the storm that just blew through, the water is unfortunately murky. The view is much more exciting in tropical waters."

Manchester was walking towards the towering window—the bottom of the ellipse kissed the floor and the top stretched just beyond his head. He stopped a few inches from the glass, and basked in the milky blue light. A smile lit his face.

Romano continued, "Douglas, your room is through the left door, and Sonali, you're on the right. This is the common area for this suite of quarters. See you at nineteen hundred in the mess for dinner. Your agenda tomorrow..." she pulled out a small, folded paper from her pocket, "ah yes, Sonali, you are meeting with the 'Farm' people and the desalination group. Douglas, you have a safety briefing and tour of *Pytheas* with James. Your mission briefing is the following morning with me. *Eccelente.* I have a few things to take care of in the lab now, but make yourselves comfortable."

"Thank you, Ryan. See you tonight," agreed Williams.

"Computer, turn down the lights," commanded Manchester still facing the window, his hands joined behind his back, pretending to be a Star Trek captain. *Tea, Earl Grey, hot.*

He turned around, "Do you think one day there will be vessels like this one travelling between the stars?"

"Well, as you know, that's partly why I'm here," said Williams. "I'm part of a NASA think-tank about how to enable *sustainable* travel between the planets. But given this fantastic boat, it looks like space exploration has a great deal to learn from ocean exploration."

"In what ways?" asked Manchester.

"International cooperation for one. I read that the crew on *Sea Orb*' is from over 15 different countries, and that the funds that allow the ship to operate year round come from a brand new United Nations program. This decouples the funding from election cycles, which has plagued NASA from the beginning. The result is scientific priorities no longer dictated by politics. What a breath of fresh air." She smiled.

"Aye," said Manchester excitedly, "Imagine what could happen if different space agencies and companies pooled resources to create a new spaceship that truly flew as an ambassador of humankind. And I know what you are thinking, but the ISS doesn't count."

The International Space Station, in low Earth orbit, had been the destination of both her space flights, and represented a stunning example of international collaboration in a climate that challenged political relationships.

Williams' mood grew more somber.

"No Doug, that's not what I was thinking. At all. I like your idealism though, but no. What you are saying will never happen, and the ISS is too tied to politics. Think about it: despite its name, the ISS remains an American product built and operated using Russian support, with small contributions by Europe and Japan. This would have to be something different. A neutral, respected entity would need to be somehow recipient of funds, similar to how the U.N. is managing *Sea Orb*." She was silent for a second, her mental gears spinning, then she threw her arms up in frustration.

"Oh, I don't know." She sighed and looked down, her hand rubbing her neck.

As her gaze shot up and pierced Manchester's, she continued, "Why would these agencies and companies pool resources if there was no return on investment? For altruistic reasons? Please Doug, it's 2027, the real world is different. Noam Chomsky said it best," and she recited from memory, "*The fate of our grandchildren counts as nothing when compared with the imperative of higher profits tomorrow.*"

Manchester felt paralyzed by her gaze, but his facial expressions changed to emotionally reach out, soothing the strain in her voice.

"For humankind to explore space, and I mean explore space for real, not land on Mars for some pictures and collect a few rocks, either something will have to happen to Earth, or the U.S. will feel its hegemony threatened by… who knows, and decide that deep space is in its national interest. Only then will we leave our cradle." she said calmly, disappointingly. "That's the nature of the society we live in."

"I didn't mean to upset you, Sonali."

Williams shook her head and started towards her room. "Nineteen hundred, Doug," she reminded. Her voice echoed in the common area as she entered her chambers and closed the door.

Manchester turned back to the window in thought, and stared in the murky distance. His hands joined behind his back, his fingers toying anxiously with his ring.

Williams' detail from NASA was to investigate how the ship maintained partial self-sufficiency. She was particularly interested in the "Farm." As an astronaut on the International Space Station, she was accustomed to pre-prepared meals. There were a few leafy greens grown for research, but the majority of the food came in freeze dried packets and required onboard rehydration. Spicy shrimp was her favorite. Because food tasted different in microgravity, the spice was welcome. They did occasionally have fresh fruit that was brought during resupply missions, but such deliveries would not be possible in deep space, at least not at the same frequency. On the ISS, the resupply capsules would be filled with trash, which, once jettisoned, would disintegrate in a planned fiery reentry through the Earth's atmosphere. This luxury would not be available to deep space travelers. Water was another topic of her investigation. As a fundamental requirement for life, water recycling would be crucial for any long-term spaceflight and would be the most valuable resource on-board. Deep-space was a formidable challenge.

The next morning, Williams was at the Farm's entrance at exactly nine. The door was closed. She knocked—no response. Williams wandered along the white-walled corridors that were lined with scientific posters showcasing the research performed on ship. She tried opening a few doors to no avail, and after ten minutes of pacing, sighed frustratingly. As she was about to leave, she heard rushed foot-steps coming closer. A short slender-looking young man emerged suddenly from a corner and jogged towards her wearing pointy leather shoes. She noticed his red socks. Half a suede scarf was flailing outside a hastily buttoned lab coat.

"*Excusez-moi*—sorry. Are you Sonali Williams?" he asked. Williams nodded. "*Très bien.* Hello. My name is Clément Cousteau. I'm a research scientist here. Doctor Romano asked me to show you our farm."

French punctuality, she nodded to herself, *and style.* "Very nice to meet you... Doctor Cousteau?" she asked puzzled. "Are you related to—

"Please call me Clément. You must come in. *Bienvenue.*" He interrupted her. Cousteau smiled, gesturing into the open door. Williams took the hint, accepted the invitation, and walked in. The sight took her by surprise; it was much larger than she had expected. The Farm was a vast room with racks filled with trays lining the walls and along the middle isle. Each rack, rising two to three times her height, contained a different plant. Rivulets of water could be heard snaking their way through the racks, but she could not quickly identify how the water was being carried. Identical dim, red LED lamps shined down on each tray; she could feel the heat as she waved her hand close to the racks. Full-spectrum artificial lighting imbued the rest of the facility.

Cousteau led her around the complex. Williams learned that red lights are actually chosen specifically to maximize growth, as that is the wavelength of the light-spectrum that is most absorbed by green plants—hence why they are green to begin with. The hydroponics setup—growth without soil—allowed some plants, such as lettuce, to be harvested "alive," without cutting the roots, so they remained fresh longer. By combining this harvest technique with immediate storage in ozonated containers, the ship's crew never had a meal without fresh vegetables. Williams was mulling about how this could be applied to microgravity, but her attention refocused when her guide started talking about water reclamation. He got halfway through his sentence, and turned around facing her.

"Are you really an astronaut?" blurted Cousteau. "That's *fantastique*. ESA is opening applications in six months. I plan on applying. I have been trained to operate the robotic arms on *Tethys*, the ROV onboard." He gestured.

Is he really miming a T. rex picking berries? she wondered amusingly.

He continued, "Today, they feel like an extension of my arms."

Williams raised an eyebrow for a second, then responded. "You should apply, you clearly have valuable knowledge and skills, but tell me, where does all the water that I hear come from?"

Cousteau straightened his back. "*Oui bien sûr*. We're surrounded by water, but of course that salt is a *problème*. The engineers who built *Sea Orb* were very conscious about water, and so deciding which technology to adopt was one of the first major decisions to be made, as the whole ship's plumbing is dependent on it. At the end of the day, vapor compression distillation was decided over reverse osmosis, because VCD can handle even the briniest, nastiest of solutions, which would clog an RO machine." He pinched his nose, then continued, "The VCD system on the lowermost deck takes in sea-water and produces the fresh water that comes out of taps and showers. That greywater is recycled through the ship first, for example by being used to flush toilets, before making it to back to the VCD system."

Williams was playing close attention.

"When you... you know..." he gestured uncomfortably, "well that blackwater is also separated by boiling. What's left is macerated with food scraps and salt and dried into fuel pellets that can burn in the furnace, which contributes to the ship's power grid. The ship is quite energy efficient. Another example..."

Manchester was following N'ksuo into the "Bay," at the bottom of the vessel. In its current submerged configuration, *Sea Orbiter II*'s base was six stories below sea level.

N'ksuo smiled. "Because the Bay's floor plan is dominated by the moonpool, we'll have to go through the airlock as the Bay is pressurized," he said. "The amount of pressurization depends on the vessel submergence and location of the Bay. The captain submerged the saucer after securing the chopper inside the ship, so right now the bay is pressurized to three bars. You'll be breathing three times the partial pressure of oxygen than you are right now. Here we go."

Manchester watched as the dial in the airlock slowly climbed from one bar, the local air pressure, to three bars, the pressure in the pressurized bay. N'kuso swung the airlock hatch open after getting the go-ahead from the green overhead light. "Welcome to my garage. Because we're actively using *Pytheas*, *Tethys*, the Remotely Operated Vehicle, is secured over there." He pointed to the blue and yellow boxy looking machine. *Tethys* had two big robotic arms secured at its front, posing as a praying mantis would prior to jumping for the kill. *Pytheas* was in the water with a ramp connecting the dripping porch to the submarine hatch.

N'kuso continued his explanation. "You are now standing in the largest marine elevator in the world. Above us is a shaft that extends to the top of the vessel. The level of the moonpool is maintained by the Bay's air pressure, so if we decrease the Bay's pressure to one bar, which we have to do when making extensive repairs, this Bay rises up towards the ceiling, pulled by powerful hydraulic jacks. At one bar, the moonpool is essentially at sea-level. This may sound cumbersome, but this means we can work and dive independently of the weather conditions outside."

"But…" started Manchester.

"I know what you're thinking, Doug. Why don't we always keep it at the one bar level? Right?"

Manchester nodded.

"For two main reasons," lectured N'kuso. "When we dive with *Tethys*, which is tethered from that winch hanging from the ceiling, we don't want to risk the cable hitting the shaft and snapping." His index finger at the tip of his extended arm traced the cable from *Tethys* up to the winch, along the ceiling to a massive pulley, and down the wall to the huge spool that took most of the floor space by the moonpool. "Thirteen kilometers of cable. Likewise, when we dive with *Pytheas*, as we will be doing tomorrow, we don't want the sub bouncing around in the shaft."

"Got it," asserted Manchester.

N'kuso stood next to the submarine. "As you can see, *Pytheas* is essentially a big titanium sphere coupled to a great deal of foam, batteries, and engines," he joked, gesturing to the submarine stoically floating behind him. Manchester's engineering mind was starting to spin.

He pointed to the open electrical box. "Why isn't the box inside the sphere? How can it sustain the pressures at depth by being outside?"

"Every inch is precious inside the sphere, so the electronics stay out. Once we've finished servicing them, silicon oil is poured in the box and the whole thing is sealed. Because oil is an incompressible fluid, it protects the electronics even at the monstrous pressures at depth."

Manchester nodded.

N'kuso talked through all the systems with Manchester, whose mind was whizzing with the satisfaction of understanding this complex ecosystem of technology. After spending a solid hour going through the external subsystems, Manchester grew giddy as N'kuso pointed towards the hatch. They climbed up the ramp, opened the hatch, and used a ladder to enter the sphere, the bottom of which was lined with Japanese tatami mats—seats would take too much vital space in the cramped sphere. They were discussing the details of the audiovisual system onboard when

Manchester casually inquired,

"Have you gotten stuck at the bottom?"

"That can't happen on my watch," laughed N'kuso, "but it is possible, I suppose. We'd have to have remained on the seafloor until all our power has drained, and even then we could drop the weights which would make *Pytheas* buoyant."

Manchester nodded again, this time silently.

"There is also the ultimate safety feature, but it's never been tested," added N'kuso as he pulled up the tatami from the curved center of the titanium floor, revealing a big bolt. "Grab me that large key behind the ladder." Manchester reached and found out a massive T-shaped wrench.

"This is our life insurance." If all else fails, with this wrench we undo that bolt, and the sphere detaches from the rest of the sub and we shoot up, out of control, and break a few bones as soon as the sphere launches out of the water and comes crashing back down on the waves. Hopefully the *Sea Orb*' isn't directly above." N'kuso was gesturing energetically.

"But…" Doug's engineering mind was again whirling.

"As I said, it's never been tested," repeated N'kuso. "Are you getting excited for our dive?" he asked.

"Aye. More than ever."

"Good morning, everyone," said Romano as stragglers plodded into the meeting room. The aroma of freshly brewed coffee filled the room. Manchester and Williams sat at the table where they had arrived five minutes early. Manchester was particularly eager to learn more about his assigned mission.

"*Sea Orb*' is now above the eastern rim of the Axial Seamount summit crater," she continued pointing the laser to the first of her slides, forming small red circles above a point on the eastern rim. "All the telemetry from the Regional Scale Nodes array indicates volcanic activity, yet the hydrophones on the ocean floor have not picked up evidence of lava erupting. These underwater microphones can pick up rocks tumbling, so it is quiet on the crater rim. The overall magnitudes of the signals these past few days have been weaker than the event three months ago. I have been in touch with seismologists in Seattle prior to this meeting, and they have concluded that the site is safe for diving. Tremors are located a safe distance away from our dive site."

Manchester leaned back, took a deep breath, and returned his hands on the table, nodding slightly. *A little ocean breeze won't keep a chopper down.*

"The opportunity of sampling the fluid vents right now is second to none," Romano boasted. After a dramatic pause, she continued, "Sensors on the seafloor are measuring increased concentrations of helium close to the vents. This means the hydrothermal waters being jetted out of the vents have high magmatic signatures and the higher temperatures of the water will most likely change the effective geochemistry."

Williams could sense her excitement rise, and a few excited whispers behind Manchester and herself signaled she was not alone in this excitement. "However," boomed Romano, "my main motivation for collecting water from the vents is fuelled by my hope that unknown bacteria, archaea, and viruses are being dislodged from the deep due to this more intense activity."

Manchester tentatively raised his hand.

"Yes, Douglas? Ah, I'm sorry, everyone, this is Douglas Manchester and Sonali Williams, from ESA and NASA respectively. We'll do introductions in a bit, what's your question?"

Whispers filled the room.

"I read a book on the plane over about a shadow biosphere, meaning a biosphere that is independent of life on Earth as we know it. Is this what is this is about?"

"In short, no, because we would not know how to look for life as we don't know it," replied Romano. She seemed thoughtful for a few seconds, before continuing, "Not with the instruments we have on ship anyway. But the essence of your question is correct, and you may be referring to Thomas Gold's book on the deep, hot biosphere rather than on a shadow biosphere, which also has been proposed?"

Manchester nodded vigorously.

Romano advocated, "Microbiologists will tell you that at the root of the tree of life, essentially the genetic 'family tree' of all life on Earth, the most primitive life forms had an affinity for hot conditions. I'm hoping that this volcanic activity may dislodge their modern cousins from their deep habitat. This would have substantial scientific value, as it would further inform which route life took in its infancy, and indicate that life is possible deep within rocks below oceans. This would be exciting for the astrobiologists who think about life on Jupiter's moon, Europa, and Saturn's moon, Enceladus. Big pharma might go crazy too, and try to make billions of dollars, like they did with a bug isolated from the hot springs of Yellowstone National Park in America."

She nodded to Manchester. "The sampling activities for tomorrow's dive is up for discussion, but here are my recommendations…"

Manchester could hardly sleep. Tomorrow morning was his turn to embark on an adventure on *Pytheas*. N'kuso, Romano, and himself were to dive one and a half miles down into a hydrothermal vent field called *International District* on the eastern rim of the Axial seamount. More specifically, they were to study *El Guapo*, a massive rock chimney made of sulfur-rich minerals spewing out superheated water at over 300°C. This had not surprised him as he knew water remained liquid despite these high temperatures because of the confining pressure.

Manchester met Romano and N'kuso for breakfast. His nose tingled to the unmistakable smell of bacon. He filled his plate with a slice of toast, seared kale, and two slices of bacon.

"Don't drink too much," warned Romano as Manchester sat with them with a big mug of tea. *Earl grey, hot.*

"Unless you wanna pee in a bottle," smirked N'kuso.

"We'll be down for about 10 hours, with no bathrooms, so hopefully your system is clear," commented Romano.

"No worries, I only had a few pints last night," grinned Manchester. Romano shrugged.

Manchester followed N'kuso and Romano out of the airlock and into the pressurized bay. The submarine was sitting in the water with the ramp leading from the bay's floor to the hatch at the top. He placed his shoes in a box at the top of the ramp, as indicated by a deck crew, and double checked he had no exposed metal. He had placed his father's ring in his pocket immediately after breakfast when Romano had reminded him of this rule.

Manchester felt a swell in his chest as he walked up the ramp, knowing whole-heartedly this was going to be a unique experience. He closed his eyes and imagined he was entering a spaceship, ready to blast off to unknown worlds. This was not far from the truth. He had been told by colleagues back in England that exploration of the seafloor in a submarine is as close as one can experience the emotions of spaceflight.

As he climbed down the ladder into the titanium sphere; the hatch closed above him. He could hear mechanisms gearing until a satisfying "click" resonated. Below him he saw N'kuso installing himself at the front, and Romano to his left, where the chief scientist typically sat. She was already studying a seafloor chart. His post was to his right.

"CO_2 scrubbers are online, and the spares are behind

you. Oxygen will be maintained at 17%. This will decrease the risk of fire, and you'll barely notice," directed N'kuso during his safety briefing. "I'm decreasing cabin pressure to one bar. This will take a bit of time."

"Where's the bottle?" joked Manchester.

"Really, Douglas?" sighed Romano.

The communication hydrophone, or comm-phone, came to life, "*Sea Orb'* to *Pytheas*, we're ready up here," echoed the voice of Williams.

"Roger, Sonali. We're completing the mechanical and electrical pre-dive checks; ETD 15 minutes," N'kuso said. After that time had passed, he gently picked up the joystick box that controlled the thrusters and robotic arms and filled the ballast tanks. *Sea Orbiter II's* deck crews signaled with thumbs up to the camera that linked the Bay to the control room, and Williams observed *Pytheas* disappearing into the water.

"Make yourself comfortable," informed N'kuso, "we have an hour before we reach the seafloor."

Manchester gazed out of his tiny port-hole; he watched the murky, green-blue water full of particles gradually turn black as *Pytheas* sank below the photic zone—the depth of water beyond which light can no longer penetrate.

Romano was busy studying her charts, while he took in what was happening to him. *Wait 'til the mates here about this*, he thought excitedly. The sonar's ping and the fan noise coming from the CO_2 scrubbers sung through the cabin. N'kuso occasionally used the comm-phone to communicate *Pytheas'* depth to *Sea Orbiter II*, followed shortly by a muffled "Roger," by Williams.

About an hour later, Manchester started noticing faint, green lights below him. They were getting progressively brighter. He felt as if he was overflying a city a night. N'kuso turned on the thrusters to slow the fall, and *Pytheas* gracefully planted on the seafloor. What he had seen were bioluminescent bacteria living throughout the solidified lava field that they lay perched upon.

Out of the port-hole, Manchester saw a crab shaking its pincers, an attempt to intimidate the strange newcomer to the ocean's depth. Manchester caught himself waving back.

"We're on the 2011 flow. Looks like we're one hundred and fifty meters from *El Guapo*, James," notified Romano.

"Yup," acknowledged N'kuso, "heading one five eight degrees North for one five zero meters". A movement of his thumbs made the submarine come to life as it lifted off the seafloor and sailed forward."

"Same ledge as usual?" proposed N'kuso.

"Yes," came Romano's reply. "We'll be able to observe the activity of *El Guapo* and decide where to sample."

N'kuso dexterously maneuvered the submarine and executed another flawless and smooth landing on the ledge. "Here we go—OH."

Pytheas lurched violently to one side.

The dive control room was humming with normality. Williams was just returning to her communications station with a freshly brewed cup of tea when, with the corner of her eye, she noticed flickering on the main control panel as the seismometers needles jumped with no apparent pattern. "What the…" she mumbled as her eyes darted across the giant flat screen at the front of the control room. The worrying stream of data coming from the seismometers was echoed from all the other instruments on the RSN array. She stood wide-eyed and perplexed.

The hydrophones recording seafloor sounds sounded with distinct bursts. A flurry of activity started as controllers actively analyzed the data to triangulate the source of the bursts.

"International District," rang a voice above the noise.

"Shit," thundered Williams as she reached for the comm-phone; her tea shattered onto the floor. "*Pytheas* abort. Abort. Axial is erupting."

"Drop the weights," bellowed Romano upon receiving Williams' message.

N'kuso flipped the trigger switches. The vessel pitched, rowed, and yawed but remained firmly anchored to the seafloor. From her vantage point, Romano could see *El Guapo* starting to violently pulsate with parts of the massive chimney disintegrating with each pulse.

"Are we recording this?" Romano asked.

"Yes, but let's get the fuck out of there," roared N'kuso still wincing out of the porthole, desperately engaging the thrusters to free their anchored sphere.

The submarine jerked again, as the crust surrounding

Pytheas cracked further, revealing the pool of molten sulfur. Manchester, as he peered wide-eyed through his porthole, felt a bead of sweat roll down his spine.

"We're draining the batteries fast; I'm stopping the thrusters," lamented N'kuso.

"What do we do now?" grieved Romano, as hope lifted away from her.

"Either we ride it out and wait for rescue, or bail," responded N'kuso.

Bail? thought Manchester

"Batteries are at 70%, or about 7 hours of power." After that, the heaters die, and we freeze to death shortly after."

Manchester lifted a tatami mat and reached out to feel the hot metal skin of the *Pytheas* before him. "Freeze? Are you sure? Feel the floor," he said.

The submarine started to gently teeter. Romano turned her camera downwards. Doug mirrored her actions. "We're floating in a pool of molten sulfur."

"Ooh, not good, not good, the electronics box is not designed for these kinds of temperatures…" N'kuso was halfway through his sentence when the lights, scrubber noises, dash displays all flickered and ceased in unison. "No," he cried as darkness swallowed the submarine.

Their only light was the glow of the lava detonating around them, dancing through the portholes, as the frigid water and scorching lava battled for supremacy of the ocean floor. As quickly as the ocean water cooled the outer shell of the lava flow to a solid crust, the increased lava and gas pressure ruptured it, destroying the crust, and causing the deafening bursts being picked up by the seafloor hydrophones.

Three flashlights turned on in the submarine, their beams battling like light sabers as the occupants of *DSV Pytheas* steadied their combined light source upon the vessel to diagnose their fate. Roiling sulfur engulfed *Pytheas'* skids, slowly entombing the vessel to the seafloor.

N'kuso reached for the T-shaped wrench.

"What are you doing?" shrieked Romano.

"Ryan, if the sulfur solidifies around the *Pytheas'* structure, we are as good as dead. No way any ship could pry us out in time. We have to do this."

N'kuso hurriedly pried off the panel and slammed the wrench on top of the fist-sized bolt.

"Doug, you're going to have to help me here." The submarine's increased rolling caused N'kuso to lose leverage.

"Hurry, Doug," barked N'kuso. He grunted as he straightened the wrench anew.

"Okay, okay, I'm ready," Manchester asserted, stabilizing himself with the opposing side of the wrench between his palms. *A little ocean breeze won't keep a chopper down.*

"On three, Doug. One, two, THREE."

THE EXPERIMENT

CRISTIAN A. SOLARI

*T*hose living in remote areas had to perform several hyperspace jumps to reach Centroid. Each cubicle sensed its visitors, setting the gravitational and atmospheric conditions to the representative's planet of origin. When fully operational, the Council of the Universe Confederation transformed into a fractal spiral network; the cubicles at the center were occupied by the representatives of the innermost Galaxies; the outer arms were occupied by the species living on the edges of the Universe. While the Council was in session, every cubicle had the chance to see, hear and feel what was taking place in the rest of the cubicles. To standardize session communications, telepathy was forbidden, all communications flowing through the Biotech Mainframe, which made the necessary translations.

Maat was one of the most prestigious mediators, and at the time in charge of the Universe Confederation Council. He was a *Talkeer*, a being with a simple organic structure, but with the capacity to communicate with any creature in the Universe. Once inside the Biotech Mainframe, the hairy structures on Maat's dorsum extended to take command of the controls, while his head initiated a pendular motion. "Fellow representatives, we have been successful in resolving conflicts remotely, but this case is quite different. That is why I have summoned you to an Extraordinary Full Presence Meeting. For the first time, one of the parties involved is not aware of the meeting, and what is worse, is not even aware of our existence, and their existence could affect us all. Most of you are familiar with the Experiment; your devices are streaming the information of the *preintelloid* civilization. The Bioframe will remain open for exchanges until we reach a decision. And so the Extraordinary Full Presence Meeting begins."

As Maat spoke, holograms of the Experiment were shown in every cubicle. "Our successful coexistence is based on our unique and succinct Constitution: *no true intelligent life form can harm in any way or interfere with another unless it is directly harmed or interfered with.* We all know the Constitution has never been broken, not even during the most complicated conflicts between diametrically opposed ways of life.

"If a new species shows up, it should be invited to become part of the Confederation. To act otherwise would be unthinkable. However, simple matters tend to shelter complex dilemmas. Our experts in intelligent life forms, Amun and Anubis, will give arguments on the matter."

It was Amun's turn; his neural centers started glowing. The Bioframe translated his mandible clicking. "In the Universe's periphery, experiments have been set up to understand the transition to high intelligence; our main hypothesis being that *intelloids* have evolved spontaneously in different parts of the Universe eons ago.

"Evolutionary rules of heritability and mutation have been fine tuned for biodiversity to flourish in the hope a lineage would eventually generate a true intelligent being. In countless experiments, life has generated spontaneously, but no true intelligent life form has ever emerged.

"In the Carbon Life Form Division, one particular experiment looked promising. We sent asteroids to collide with the planet of interest to change important environmental parameters so the lineage which seemed to have the potential to evolve intelligence could radiate, and displace the dead-end ones. To everybody's surprise, the experiment succeeded and self-conscious *preintelloids* evolved and became the dominant species in the planet. The Experiment was considered the most successful in history, the first to spontaneously develop a sophisticated, pre-intelligent life form."

As Amun continued, his tentacles formed smooth metachronal waves, "We now face the dawn of a new civilization, with complex self-conscious individuals, but still with many primitive traits. What we would have never expected was that their space travel technology would go so far in this stage of their evolution. It took longer for many of the civilizations represented in this meeting to develop hyperspace accelerators. In a short time they were able to develop the technology that might allow them to meet their creators, us. Nevertheless, it is my opinion that if *preintelloids* master hyperspace travel, we should give them the chance to join our Confederation."

Data and images were streaming from the Sociological Development Hub and the Evolutionary Ecology Hub: the databases that informed resource management. The evolutionary ecology indicators showed that *preintelloids* had been learning to optimize their resources. The colonization of their star system and settlements had helped them improve resource utilization. Their achievements had been significant, but when analyzing the data, Council members could observe that *preintelloids* were still some steps away from *intelloid* status. Selfishness, aggressive interactions, and ownership disputes were still driving forces in their civilization.

"I fully understand that we would be taking risks, as they still show signs of aggressive behavior. But *preintelloids* are also on the brink of becoming fully cooperative. It is unconceivable not to apply the Constitution, even if they are not fully developed."

Amun ceded the floor to his research colleague, Anubis, whose mandibles started clicking. "Fellow representatives, our Confederation is in danger. Have we gone too far? Some may argue it was unthinkable to consider that a civilization could master hyperspace travel without reaching a cooperative evolutionary state. Was it really unthinkable? An experiment that goes out of control must be terminated."

Amun addressed the Council again. "We still do not know how much of the aggressive behavior is innate or acquired by cultural evolution. The transition to full cooperation might be imminent."

Anubis' neural centers were glowing intensely. "But it

could take a long time to understand the heredity mecha-nisms of this trait. Competitive aggressive behavior, high reproduction rate, and intergalactic travel are the three characteristics that turn *preintelloids* into a possible men-ace to the Universe as a whole. The potential expanding species could be in the near future migrating to systems populated by *intelloids* living in harmony and respectful of each other and the Constitution. The Experiment must be terminated immediately. Anytime, *preintelloids* may show up in one of our worlds. We can only hope they will act as any of us would.

"Nevertheless," Anubis continued, "the Constitution does not apply in this case. Most *preintelloids* still have the competitive aggressive behavior; a behavior that none of the members of the Universe Confederation has. For a spe-cies to be considered intelligent, all of its members must be fully cooperative. Thus, our Constitution does not protect them. They are *preintelloids*, not *intelloids*."

The representatives' opinions in the Bioframe went from unequivocally respecting the Constitution to abruptly in-terrupting the course of the *preintelloids'* evolution. They felt awkward, wrestling between two unnatural choices. As he checked the Bioframe, Maat's hair-like sensors detected that many of the representatives were convinced by Anu-bis's arguments, especially as his words made them aware of the grave decision they had to make. But all of them were still strongly tied to the Constitution. They found it difficult to consider the possibility of exterminating anyone who might be close to becoming an intelligent being. It was embedded, imprinted in their foundations. *Preintelloids* were close to reaching *intelloid* status, but it was impossible to calculate a time frame for the transition.

Maat intervened, "Fellow representatives, someone from the outer rim has requested to directly address the Council. Please proceed."

"Fellow representatives, we should not fix a mistake with another one. The termination will unbalance our peaceful existence. We have to take responsibility for the risks that we took when we approved these experiments. Let *preintelloids* evolve. Yes, they could threaten eons of harmony in the Universe, but it is not their fault, it is ours.

"As *preintelloids*, we are one of the few carbon-based species in the Confederation. As you can all see, convergent evolution has made their morphology and neural network similar to ours, although our star-system is far away from the Experiment. *Preintelloids* are special to us and we feel a deep connection to them. As representatives of the Human species, we ask the Council to appoint us Guardians of the *preintelloid* civilization, making us fully responsible for the Experiment and its star-system as a whole. We would commit all the resources necessary to monitor the emergent civilization and immediately report to the Council any threat or problem that might arise. We would not allow any spaceship to leave their star-system until the Council dictates that they are ready to meet us all."

As everybody else, Maat was surprised at the proposal. *Humans* were willing to take full charge of The Experiment to save these primitive creatures. As members resumed sending input to the Bioframe, what had until then been a small ripple from a remote civilization became a giant wave that flooded the entire fractal network. "We are all *Humans*" resonated on the Bioframe, and spread like a virus. The Bioframe's only output was "*Humans*." Nothing of what had happened changed Anubis' mind, but the decision was, as always, unanimous. The termination was postponed.

This was not an experiment anymore, Maat thought. Individual molecular transporters materialized each of the representatives into their hyperspace transport systems, leaving the Council empty. As he watched the spaceships disappear into oblivion, Maat hoped that Randomness would not challenge the Universe Confederation like this again. He knew that an empty Council meant a successful Universe Confederation.

Liked what you read? Stay in touch with us!

Follow the Blue Marble Space Institute of Science on Twitter **@BlueMarbleSpace**, or send an email to **info@bmsis.org**.

Join SAGANet at **saganet.org** and share your thoughts about science, philosophy, fiction, and the future.

Follow Habitable Press on Twitter **@HabitablePress** for updates on upcoming publications.

ABOUT THE AUTHORS

Logan Brenner holds an M.A. in earth & environmental sciences. He lives in Philadelphia, Pennsylvania.

Simon Gonzalez holds a Ph.D. in biological & biomedical sciences. He lives in San Antonio, Texas.

Nathan Fredrickson holds a master of social work. He lives in Lawrence, Kansas.

Jacob Haqq-Misra holds a Ph.D. in meteorology & astrobiology. He lives in Clayton, Delaware.

Ian Jaymes holds degrees in biology and political science. He lives in Santa Clara, California.

Ivan Glaucio Paulino-Lima holds a Ph.D. in biophysics. He lives in Mountain View, California.

W. Richardson holds degrees in astrophysics and biology. She lives in Boulder, Colorado.

Crystal Riley holds an M.S. in computer science. She lives in San Francisco, California.

Shaelyn Silverman holds a B.A. in biology & neuroscience. She lives in Saratoga, California.

Sanjoy M. Som holds a Ph.D. in planetary sciences & astro-biology. He lives in Sunnyvale, California.

Cristian A. Solari holds a Ph.D in ecology & evolutionary biology. He lives in Argentina.